WARNING

This book contains sexually explicit scenes and adult language. It may be considered offensive to some readers. This book is for sale to adults ONLY.

* * * * * * * * * * * * * * * * *

Please store your files wisely where they cannot be accessed by underage readers.

ISBN-13: 978-1773500560
ISBN-10: 1773500562

Other books by Shyla Starr:

<u>Tenacious Billionaire BWWM Romance Series</u>

Adalia is too proud to accept help from the billionaire playboy, Trent Dawson. How long can she maintain her resolve? The bank is at her heels to repossess her business. To make matters worse, Adalia finds suspicious evidence of Trent's philandering ways. She must determine whether to trust Trent with the fate of her business and her heart.

<u>Elusive Billionaire Romance Series</u>

Billionaire Hendrick is trying to repair his company's image by putting in some volunteer work, building a school and hospital for the impoverished children in Africa. There, he meets a beautiful African American volunteer, Jocelyn. They hit it off right away but does she belong in his world?

<u>Lonely Billionaire Romance Series</u>

Tricia was hired to care for billionaire John's wife, who is dying. An unlikely romance emerges after his wife, Rebecca, gives John permission to pursue his happiness after she is gone.

<u>Ardent Billionaire Romance Series</u>

Deirdre doesn't know what to make of the gorgeous man that seems to be interested in her. His name is Parker Walters and he seems friendly enough. There is just something off about him. Why is he trying the hide the fact that he is the heir to his father's billion dollar software empire?

Fervent Billionaire BWWM Romance Series

Alexandra had never been with a white man before. She had seen William at the café before but she always kept her distance. It was unfortunate that their first chance meeting happened when she dropped her breakfast and spilled coffee all over his expensive business suit.

Audacious Billionaire BWWM Romance Series

Chante is torn between staying close to a man beyond her league, and fleeing from him to spare herself from a hopeless position. But she finds she is propelled into a place where she needs to confront her doubts and cast her fate aside to follow the dictates of her heart. Damned if she does and miserable is she doesn't, how will Chante face the events that will lead her to a place of pure happiness or to the pits of a broken heart?

Get the latest update on new releases from the author at:

https://shylastarr.com/newsletter/

This book is Part Two of the "Persuasive Billionaire BWWM Romance Series"

1 - Love Invested

Stacey is trying to keep a handle on her life the best that she can. She is on the verge of losing her job and her apartment, while taking care of her sick grandmother. Her life takes an unexpected turn when she meets Charlie, who works for the construction company that is attempting to persuade her to move out of her home.

2 - Love Divested

After discovering that Charlie has a fiancée, Stacey's world has turned upside down. She cannot help but feel as if she is in over her head. Struggling with her job, her bills and her family, will Stacey be able to figure out how she can get her life straightened out?

3 - Love Reinstated

Stacey decides that she has to put Charlie behind her and move on with her life. As Stacey dates Tony and is pulled into his world, she slowly realizes that although she likes him, it might not be enough to brush aside her feelings for Charlie. Leaving everything behind, she lets herself get lost in the money and privacy that Tony brings to her.

4 - Love Confirmed

Stacey can't believe the turn of events in her life. After losing her grandmother and running away to Tony's private island, she was content to stick her head in the sand and forget her past. But a proposal from Charlie changes everything.

5 - Love Divine

Stacey must ensure she relaxes in order to keep her baby safe. But life is never that easy. Her new husband's father is bent on sabotaging their fledgling investment firm. To make things worse, her brother-in-law isn't content with just being in the background. Stacey finds herself wishing she could have the brothers patch things up.

Persuasive Billionaire BWWM Romance Series

Love Divested

Book Two

By Shyla Starr

Table of Contents

Chapter One

DOWNSTAIRS IN the lobby, Stacey saw a woman who was, clearly, not a tenant. The stranger looked like she belonged in a fashion magazine.

Trying to be helpful, Stacey asked, "Hi, are you lost?"

The woman looked Stacey up and down before answering. "Yes, I believe so. I'm looking for someone."

"Who are you looking for?"

"Charlie Albert. He had business here before he mucked up the deal. Have you seen him?"

Stacey's heart raced. "Uh, no. No, not for a few days. Who are you?" It was a bit blunt, but she couldn't help herself. Who was this woman?

The woman lowered her glasses and replied, "I'm Charlie Albert's fiancée, not that it's any business of yours."

Stacey thought she misheard the woman. There had to be some sort of mistake. There was no way that this woman was Charlie's fiancée.

"I'm Adele," the woman went on, oblivious to Stacey's inner turmoil. "I wanted to surprise him, you see. I've been overseas. His assistant said he had been here a couple times, so I thought he could be here now."

"Sorry, he hasn't been here since the apartments were dropped from the rebuilding plan." Stacey hoped her voice sounded as if she had no interest in Adele or her claims of being Charlie's fiancée.

Adele wrinkled her nose. "That's a shame. I suppose I'll try him elsewhere then. Now that I'm here, though, I can understand why he would leave as quickly as possible." She laughed.

Stacey wanted to tell this strange, uppity woman that this was her home. She didn't need strangers coming around running their mouths off about how little they thought of it. But she couldn't bring herself to say anything. Instead, she could only stare at Adele, who was looking around the lobby one last time.

"Well, thank you for the help, dear," Adele said and left the apartment complex in her towering high heels without a backward glance.

Stacey just stood there. Her head was spinning as if everything had suddenly been uprooted. Part of her wanted to chase after Adele and ask her just how she could be Charlie's fiancée.

But a sick, swooping feeling was slowly consuming Stacey. She had to talk to Charlie as soon as possible. She fumbled for her phone and brought up his number. The phone rang three times before a man answered.

"Charlie Albert's phone." The man's voice was deep and somehow familiar although it wasn't Charlie.

No one had ever picked up Charlie's cell phone before and it threw Stacey off guard. She stumbled over her words. "Hi, uh, hello. This is Stacey, and, um, I'm Charlie's—" What was she, exactly? His girlfriend? Or just a girl on the side?

"Stacey!" the man exclaimed as if he knew her. "This is Tony."

In her haze, it took her a few seconds to remember who Tony was. The image of him smiling at her on board his yacht floated back to Stacey.

"Right, hi Tony!" She feigned a cheerfulness. "How are you? Your yacht was very lovely."

"Glad you enjoyed it. I enjoyed seeing you on it."

The remark startled her. His tone had been warm and almost flirtatious. That's odd, she thought to herself.

"I'm calling for Charlie," she blurted out and cringed.

She probably sounded incredibly rude. She was blowing off what Tony had just said. But Stacey had no idea what to make of it and couldn't focus on that right now. The image of smug Adele still danced in her memory.

"He's in a meeting. He's running late, actually, because we had a meeting of our own. That's how I have his phone," Tony joked, "but I can pass him a message."

"Yeah, please. Let him know I called and would appreciate a call back."

"Of course. I had no idea you two were so, well, close," Tony replied tactfully.

For one wild second, Stacey wanted to ask Tony about Adele. He would know, wouldn't he? Tony and Charlie seemed to be friends and ran in the same social circles. But she stopped herself before she could do something so silly. No, whatever was going on was something she would ask Charlie directly. She would not go behind his back.

"Thank you! I have to go to work now. Have a nice day!" Her voice was too high-pitched as she tried to hide her emotions. It just made her sound crazy and somewhat desperate.

She ended the call and headed to work, telling herself that she would get to the bottom of it soon enough.

Although Stacey had promised herself not to dwell on Charlie and Adele, it proved to be impossible. The restaurant had one lone customer—an old lady sitting at a booth asking for coffee non-stop as she read a book.

Maria bustled into the kitchen about two hours into her shift and looked over at Stacey. "I quit."

"What? That just leaves me and Amanda."

Maria shrugged. "Not my problem. I'm going to go fucking mental if I stay here a second longer. See you around."

Stacey stared as Maria headed toward the break room. She hadn't ever been exactly close with Maria so she hadn't been expecting a tearful goodbye. But a mumbled 'see you around' was a pretty shitty farewell.

Tears formed in Stacey's eyes. She turned away to face the wall. *What is wrong with me?* She tried to regroup. Normally, someone quitting wouldn't affect her like this.

She left the kitchen, leaving Brad behind playing a game on his phone and found William in his office. She knocked on the door, and he looked up at her.

"You're not quitting too, are you? I was hoping to run with a skeleton crew until we closed, but it's turning more into a ghost crew at this point."

"Nope, I'm here 'til we close," Stacey replied. "I have a job lined up afterward already."

"Amanda mentioned that the other day. Congrats."

Working at another diner didn't seem like something to be congratulated about. Out of the blue, her sister's words from their last fight haunted her. *All you do is work at some dead-end job without ever trying to better yourself or move onto something new.*

"Thanks," Stacey replied without really meaning it. "Figured I'd see if you wanted to alter the schedule."

"I can't give you any more hours. You're already in overtime on my end. I'll pick up some shifts. You know, Stacey, if you are hurting for money, I'd understand if you have to leave early."

She was touched that William was giving her a way out if she wanted to take it. William had always paid everyone more than the minimum wage plus tips for wait staff. She didn't need much, and it had always been enough to scrape by. Business had been so slow lately that the tips barely made a dent in her bills. But she was determined to stay out of loyalty to an employer who had treated her well the last four years.

"I'm making due," she replied.

William looked relieved, "Thanks, Stacey. Don't worry about Maria quitting. I'll take care of it."

"Just wanted to make sure. Thanks," Stacey said and left the office with a wave.

She had been secretly hoping to get Maria's hours. Not only because she wanted the money but because she had been hoping if she threw herself into her job then she could forget about everything else on her mind.

William had reminded her of another thing bothering her—her foolish sister and that damned diamond tennis bracelet. Allison had promised to give her the bracelet after dragging her to the yacht party.

Instead, she had given it back to Jacob when he left for Europe in some misguided attempt at being romantic.

That was Allison in a nutshell. She would make promises and deals and never follow through with them. She'd change things at the last second on any whim. Stacey should have seen it coming. When she thought about how much they could have fetched selling that bracelet, it made her sick. She closed her eyes for a few seconds. Then she went to go check on her lone coffee-guzzling customer.

Charlie didn't call her back until late in the afternoon when she was almost done with her shift. When her phone vibrated in her pocket, she slunk off to the break room to take the call. Amanda had shown up twenty minutes ago, so Stacey finally had help to cover the customers.

"Hey, sorry it took me so long to call you back," Charlie said when she answered.

"It's fine. I need to talk to you about something."

"Can it wait until tonight when I see you? There're a few urgent matters I need to tend to in a few minutes."

Stacey was taken aback. She was just going to confront him over the phone about Adele and had forgotten about their date later in the evening. But in person was probably better where she could watch his reaction.

"Oh, that's what I'm calling about. I have to run an important errand for Tina tonight. Can we meet up for coffee or something instead?" Stacey felt there was no point in prolonging the agony over a dinner.

"Yeah, sure." Charlie's voice sounded disappointed.

She gave him the name of a coffee place near her apartment complex, and he said he would meet her there at six.

The rest of Stacey's shift dragged by. She was incredibly nervous about seeing Charlie. She finished work with twenty minutes to get to the coffee shop. She tried to fix herself up before leaving to see him.

I shouldn't waste my time, she told herself as she reapplied her lipstick. *Why bother primping for him?* Even so, Stacey ran a brush through her hair and set off to see him.

Chapter Two

Charlie was waiting when Stacey arrived. He had chosen a table in the back of the coffee shop. The place served run-of-the-mill coffee, but it was the only nearby place Stacey could afford. Charlie was on his phone and hadn't seen her yet.

She stood there for a few seconds admiring him. He was handsome, and she liked looking at him. He was still dressed in business attire, probably from coming directly from the office. Stacey imagined his days were busy with a thousand different things going on at once. Perhaps, in another life, it could have worked out between them. But they were too different.

Stacey steeled herself and walked over to him, not bothering to buy a coffee. She was going to keep this short by telling him she had met his fiancée and couldn't see him anymore. She sat down across from him.

"Didn't even see you there," Charlie said, smiling. "Sorry again for missing your call earlier. At least Tony got it. Work has been hectic today."

"I can imagine," Stacey replied, trying to sound casual, "especially with Adele flying in."

Charlie stiffened. He was about to reach for his coffee but his hand froze. He was thrown off balance but Stacey found no pleasure in it. She just felt tired.

"Adele is in town?" he finally asked after swallowing a few times.

"Yup, she stopped by the complex, thinking you might be there. She didn't care much for the place though. Made it pretty clear that she thought it was gross."

"Sounds like her," Charlie said with a sigh.

Stacey drummed her fingers against the table, waiting for him to say more. Her gaze must have unnerved him because he leaned forward.

"She isn't my fiancée, Stacey."

"Really?" Her tone was clipped.

He sighed and ran his fingers through his hair, "Let me explain. My father organized the stupid engagement. He thinks it's good for me to be paired with Adele. Her family owns a huge media company overseas. Dad wants to merge with them."

"Don't you control the company though?"

"Yeah, but only because my father is too ill to keep running it," Charlie replied. "I took over the company a few years ago. Dad is constantly going behind my back, still trying to control things. But he's too sick to manage the company properly. Lately, his schemes just keep getting more and more out of control. And my brother, Eric, sides with him on absolutely everything. He's furious he didn't get to run things so anything he can do to fuck things up for me, he jumps right on board."

Stacey held up her hand. "So, you're trying to tell me that your father planned this engagement with Adele behind your back? Do you think I'm stupid? Why would I believe that?"

"You can't honestly believe I'd be seeing you if I were engaged to Adele!" he exclaimed.

"You haven't exactly been up front this entire time, Charlie."

"I know that but I thought—I thought I made things right. After changing my plans about the city."

"You did. You did make things right," Stacey replied, feeling guilty.

He had changed all his plans, hadn't he? He had come to her with a new business plan just so people didn't have to worry about leaving their homes. Stacey knew that he had gone out on a limb for all the residents, for her.

Charlie saw her weakening resolve and kept speaking, "My father really wants me to marry Adele. I've only met her a handful of times. She's in it for the money. I have no interest in being with her, not for a moment and certainly not in marriage."

"But she's going around telling people that you two are engaged. How can I just stand by while another woman does that?"

"I'll make it clear to her that we aren't together. I'll make it right. I'll tell her you and I are together. You can even be there if you want to see it for yourself." Charlie was pleading now. "Let me show you I have nothing to hide, Stacey."

She was wavering and Charlie could feel it. He had those puppy dog eyes again. Staring into them, she could believe that maybe everything would work out after all. He was offering to tell Adele to back off in front of her. Would someone be willing to do that, not to mention change his business plan for her?

"Fine," she heard herself say.

A smile broke across Charlie's face, "Great. I didn't even know Adele was here. She's probably waiting for me at my apartment. Come with me. We can end this now."

He stood up and held out his hand to hers. Stacey hesitated for only a moment before taking it.

Stacey had never been to Charlie's apartment before. It was near the beach in the section of town she had very rarely visited. His apartment was the penthouse of his building which was so close to the beach she could have walked to it every day if she felt like it.

The entrance had a fountain in the center, spilling out bright blue water. The lobby was otherwise silent, with the receptionist typing away at her laptop. The marble flooring was spotless and shined under the low lights. Stacey couldn't help but marvel at the difference between this lobby and the one back home. This one was so big it could have fit more than two of her apartments.

Charlie grabbed Stacey's hand, sensing her nerves, as he slid his keycard into a slot by the elevator.

"Fancy," she joked as an attempt to hide the butterflies in her stomach.

He shot her a smile and together they took the elevator up to the thirtieth floor. The doors opened silently directly to Charlie's penthouse. Stacey's breath caught.

The hallway opened into the living room which had a fantastic view of the ocean. The sun was setting and the fading light spilled across the ocean which glittered like a gem. She was so caught up by the view that she didn't even hear Adele's heels clattering down the hallway.

"You're home! Finally! I've been waiting to surprise you for ages!" Her voice rang out as she came around the corner and stopped at the sight of Stacey.

Charlie pulled Stacey forward, across the threshold of the apartment. Adele's gaze flicked to Stacey as confusion crossed her face.

"What is someone from that God-awful apartment complex doing here?"

"Adele, you should have told me you were coming," Charlie said firmly, pulling Stacey along with him as they walked into his living room. "So I could have told you not to bother."

Adele scoffed, "What's gotten into you?"

"Nothing new," he remarked, pulling out his cell phone. "What hotel would you like to stay at?"

"I'm not staying at any hotel. I'm staying here!" she snapped.

For the first time, Stacey saw hard iron beneath Adele's lovely features. Without the giant sunglasses to hide her face, Adele's face was fully exposed. She was beautiful, skinny, and tall like a model. She was still wearing the outfit from earlier in the day but now her hair was down, cascading over her shoulders. Her hair was sleek and shiny as if she had just stepped off a photo shoot for a shampoo commercial. Her green eyes were gorgeous, lined in perfectly applied eye make-up. Her red painted lips were kissable and plump.

Standing across from such a woman, Stacey felt fat and hideous. She suddenly regretted agreeing to come here. Charlie didn't seem to be in awe of Adele's beauty, however. He just looked irritated.

"No, you're not. Tell my father you're going back home. Give him back that horrible ring too." He

gestured to an incredibly large diamond ring that Adele
was wearing.

"Who is this?" Adele pointed to Stacey.

"This is my girlfriend," Charlie said.

"What?" Adele went slack-jawed for a brief
moment before glaring. "Surely, this is a joke? What
are you doing, slumming for fun now?"

Her words were like a slap in the face. It woke
Stacey up from the nervous fog that had enveloped her.
She took a determined step toward Adele.

"Apparently money can't buy manners or human
decency."

Charlie snickered at Stacey's remark, which just
seemed to anger Adele more. She turned to look at
Charlie.

"You must really want to piss your father off," she
snapped. "If you think he's going to be okay with
this—" she pointed to Stacey as if she was a stray dog,
"instead of me, you are sadly mistaken."

"Dad doesn't call the shots anymore, Adele.
Whatever he promised you or told you would happen,
isn't going to happen. I'm not marrying you. So, please
leave."

Adele looked as if she had been slapped in the face.
Then she snatched her purse off the couch. As she
turned to leave, she paused and looked back at Stacey.

"This isn't over."

Then she left, storming out of the penthouse, with Stacey watching. Her heart was beating fast. Sure, Charlie had told Adele off, but it didn't seem to matter too much to her.

"That, uh, sort of went well," Stacey remarked once the coast was clear.

Charlie sighed and closed his eyes for a moment. "That woman gives me a headache."

"How long have you known her?" Stacey asked.

"About four years now. Shortly after I was given control of the company, my father threw a birthday party for me. She was there. I could tell right away he had been scheming behind my back because she knew too many private details about me."

"Why does she want to marry you so badly?"

"Money. Her family is loaded but not as loaded as mine. She loves the lifestyle. This isn't the first time I've told her the engagement isn't happening but my father, brother, and Adele don't care what I think or how I feel."

"That sounds insane, sorry," Stacey said, sitting down on the couch, "I mean, all of this is overwhelming."

It was. The more she learned about Charlie, the more she realized just how far out of her league she was. She had thought dealing with Allison's quest to snag a billionaire was silly and over the top. But Charlie had his own family plotting against him to wed some woman who only wanted his riches. He owned a company worth billions of dollars and had probably been around the world more times than she could count.

Meanwhile, Stacey was excited simply to have found another diner job before her current place of employment closed down. She was happy if she found an extra five-dollar bill in her purse.

They came from two different universes and she was suddenly terrified.

Charlie sat down next to her and grabbed her hand, "You alright?"

"Yeah. Well, no. Not really. This is all pretty crazy, Charlie. I don't know. I had thought once you spoke to Adele, I'd feel better but…" she trailed off.

"Maybe this will help," Charlie whispered.

He leaned over and brought his lips to hers. Stacey could feel the electric charge surge over her as soon as they touched. She still wasn't used to that. She had never been around anyone who could simply kiss her and bring her to life like that.

The kiss deepened. It had been a long time since that day they had been alone and Stacey felt it acutely. It was like she had been suppressing an urge this entire time. Now Charlie had stirred it again, and it was clawing to get out.

His hands were on the side of her face, pulling her toward him as he slid his tongue into her mouth. Stacey's own hands were running through his hair. She could feel his heart beating wildly in his chest, matching her own heartbeat.

She pulled him down on top of her on the couch. He was overdressed, Stacey thought as she loosened his clothes. Charlie, sensing what she wanted, slipped out of his suit jacket and tossed it to the floor.

"Here?" he whispered.

"Anywhere," she replied quietly.

Charlie didn't hold back after her urging. He unbuttoned his dress shirt, and it dropped to the floor as Stacey pulled off her own t-shirt. Would she ever grow tired of drinking in the sight of Charlie? He was so toned and perfectly built. She ran her fingers down his chest and pulled him toward her again for another kiss.

Their mouths smashed together as he yanked her pants off. Every nerve of hers was alert, wanting and needing more of him. Soon, they were both naked. As she felt his hot skin press against hers, she sighed and closed her eyes. Even feeling him just like this was almost enough—almost.

He parted her thighs and ran his fingers along her wet pussy. It caused her to shiver. Here they were, too impatient to even go to his room to fuck. The thought thrilled her. She loved that they needed each other this badly.

Charlie slid one finger inside of her and began to move it slowly. Stacey let out a soft moan and tried to move her hips, silently begging him for more. Charlie refused. Instead, his movements were slow and languid. The one finger wasn't enough, and he knew it. But he still dragged every motion out just to torture her. She took hold of his erect member and slid her hand up and down the hot shaft.

Before she could say anything or beg him for more, he shifted so he was on the floor of the living room. He pulled her down with him in his strong arms. Their lips clashed together again. She could feel how quickly his heart was beating underneath her fingertips. He dragged his bottom lips against her lips, grazing them gently.

His fingers found her pussy again. He slid them inside of her and began to pump them quickly, in and out of her wetness. Stacey gasped and writhed underneath him. His lips found her neck, and he darted his tongue against her warm skin. All she could do was hold onto him as he finger-fucked her hard and fast.

She could feel her own orgasm mounting. But just as she thought she was going to topple over the edge, Charlie's fingers slid up her belly. She gasped in surprise and annoyance. But before she could say anything, Charlie was shifting down toward her thighs.

He left butterfly kisses the entire way down and then his tongue flicked across her pussy. Stacey arched her back. Each movement of Charlie's tongue was enough to almost send her to climax—almost. He seemed to gauge just when to stop, to keep her from finishing.

Ultimately, the mixture of his tongue and fingers proved to be too much. Stacey climaxed right on his living room couch. Charlie held onto her thighs. His fingers dug into her skin as he flicked his tongue gently against her clit as she came.

As her orgasm finished, leaving her warm all over, she realized just how much she wanted to taste Charlie. She got to her knees and pushed him to the floor.

He sensed what she was going to do and whispered her name, "Stacey."

She dragged her tongue up his cock as slowly as she could bear it. It throbbed underneath her tongue as she wrapped her lips around the head. Charlie moaned. The sound of his pleasure encouraged her. She rolled her tongue around the head of his cock and then tried to fit as much of him as she could into her mouth. Her other hand cupped his balls, gently moving them around.

Charlie was gasping from the sensation of her tongue around his hard shaft. Stacey liked the taste of him—there was a mixture of sweet and salty that filled her mouth as she sucked.

After a few minutes, Stacey stopped. She wanted to feel him inside of her. She climbed on top of him and positioned his cock so he could easily slide inside of her. Charlie grabbed her hips as she lowered herself onto him.

She couldn't help it—she let out a loud moan. She was glad he lived in the penthouse because there was no way anyone next door wouldn't have heard them. Stacey began to ride him. Charlie's hands massaged her breasts, and he pinched her nipples lightly. He rolled her tits around in his hands as she buried her pussy around his cock.

Stacey closed her eyes and focused on how completely wonderful everything felt. She could hear their skin smacking together. She could feel his cock pounding inside of her with each thrust. Charlie's hands slid to her hips and down along her skin.

Before she could climax again, he gripped her waist tightly and yanked her down on top of him. She was pressed against Charlie. Their skin was slick with sweat. Her own heart fluttered in her chest. Charlie held her hips so that she couldn't move.

Then he began to thrust into her pussy hard and fast. From this position, her clit was grinding against his shaft. The movement of his cock thrusting inside of her and her clit being rubbed was too much.

Stacey let out a loud moan and climaxed. She was pressed against Charlie and couldn't move. She let the orgasm engulf her. Charlie grunted and thrust inside her one last time before he shuddered.

They came together, clutching each other as they rocked. Stacey, having her second orgasm so quickly, felt this one was even more intense than the first. By the time it ended, she was completely out of breath.

Charlie held onto her. He was out of breath as well and had his eyes closed. Stacey looked at him. He opened his eyes and looked at her. Then he brought her in for a kiss. She could taste herself on him mixed with the saltiness of their skin. She liked it.

He pressed his forehead against hers and murmured something. It sounded like her name. They held each other like this, on the floor of his penthouse. They were in no hurry. There was nothing to bother them here. Stacey couldn't have moved even if she wanted to. Like the last time they slept together, her limbs felt heavy. Her eyelids were trying to close as if they wanted to explore dreams.

She let herself stay like this for a while, enjoying Charlie holding her. It had been a long time since she had connected like this sexually with anyone. *Why rush it?*

When Charlie pulled her in for another round, there was no way Stacey was going to refuse, no matter what her silly eyelids wanted.

Chapter Three

"Where were you?" Allison asked when Stacey got home later that night.

"Stayed late to help cover a shift," she lied, thinking swiftly.

Normally, her sister wouldn't have questioned her. But maybe it was because she was still upset about Jacob going off to Europe without her. Maybe Allison found an excuse to be angry with Stacey who was still pissed off that she had given back the tennis bracelet. Stacey wouldn't have put it past her.

"Really?" Allison drawled.

"Where is Tina?"

"In here, dear!" her grandmother called from the kitchen.

"Come here." Allison motioned with her hand.

Stacey went over to her sister and sat down next to her. She wasn't in the mood to fight or get asked a thousand different questions about why she was late.

"Something happened earlier today with Tina."

Stacey blinked. She hadn't been expecting anything to do with her grandmother. She suddenly felt nervous.

"What happened?"

"She forgot where she was for like, a good five minutes. I managed to help her until her memory came back but… Stacey, you can't keep her here. She needs care. Actual care by a nurse or something. It's only a matter of time until she hurts herself or something bad happens when we aren't here."

Stacey opened her mouth to protest. It was a knee-jerk reaction when it came to Tina. But Allison anticipated this and cut her off.

"Listen to me. Just listen to me," she said in a harsh voice. "I'm not trying to play the bitch here. But we must consider other arrangements because she can't stay here, Stacey. I know you want to take care of her but you can't, alright? She needs a doctor and medical attention."

"I can't afford it," Stacey snapped, feeling defensive. "I'm doing what I can, alright? You don't just get to swoop in here and start telling me what to do."

"I'm not swooping in here and telling you what to do. I'm thinking about our grandmother. She's only going to get worse. You and I both know that."

"What do you propose I do? I can't afford a nurse or to send her to a home. I can barely afford to make ends meet now."

"Get another job then. Work two jobs. Didn't you say you wanted to get an office job? Keep looking."

Something about her sister's tone irritated her. Maybe it wasn't just Allison. Even after being with Charlie earlier today, Stacey was still worried she was in over her head with him and his life. On top of that, she had to worry about everything else going on like work and her grandmother. Coming home to find Allison on the couch, telling her that she wasn't doing enough for Tina and needed to get another job, pushed her over the edge.

"I wouldn't have to worry about any of that if you had just kept your promise about the tennis bracelet," Stacey snapped.

Allison's eyes widened in an attempt at looking innocent, "You're still upset about that?"

"It only happened this morning!"

"I said I was sorry! You'll get the bracelet when Jacob comes back."

"If he even wants to see you again," Stacey hissed.

Allison looked irritated, "Don't start with that shit. Don't take it out on me that our grandmother is sick and needs better care."

"So, why don't you help, then? You know, for all the gold digging you do, Tina hasn't seen a penny of it. Must be nice to come in here and tell me what to do when you don't have to put a cent toward fixing problems!"

Allison looked furious but Stacey stood up to march out of the room. She had no interest in whatever her sister had to say to defend herself. As she headed toward her room, Allison delivered one last parting shot.

"You should take a shower, sis, because you smell like sex."

That brought her up short for a moment. She debated turning around but knew it would just feed into what her sister wanted. Instead, Stacey stormed off into her room.

Once she closed the bedroom door, tears sprung to her eyes. Today had been overwhelming to deal with. Too many things had happened. Between fighting with Allison, the loss of the tennis bracelet, and everything going on with Charlie, she wanted to just curl up in a ball.

The worst part of it? Allison was right. Her grandmother did need a nurse and additional medical care. But she just couldn't afford it. She didn't want to shove Tina in some awful place. She wanted the best for her. But Stacey couldn't afford it.

She couldn't sit around and rely on Allison handing over some diamonds she snagged from a rich guy. She had to take matters into her own hands. That included doubling her efforts to find a better paying job rather than settling for another waitress job.

Stacey took a shuddering breath and successfully warded off the flood of tears. No, she wasn't going to cry. Allison would have loved that. If Tina was getting worse, then she needed Allison to stay there to keep an eye on things. As much as she would love to kick her sister to the curb, she needed her.

She heard the shower turn on in the bathroom down the hall. Knowing the coast was clear from her sister, Stacey left her room to grab something quick to eat. Tina was at the dining room table with a sandwich in front of her and an old paperback book next to the plate.

"Hey," Stacey said to Tina, going over to kiss her on the top of her head.

"How was your day, dear?"

"Good, good. Everything is going well," Stacey said swiftly.

Her grandmother nodded although her eyes looked distant, "Well, that's good."

"Maria quit today. She just left. Barely even said goodbye. I know no one is in love with the diner, but I couldn't just quit and not even say goodbye, you know?"

"Yes, yes."

Stacey looked at her grandmother. Tina was still staring at her, but her response and the distant look in her eyes made it clear that she hadn't been following the discussion. That was the case more and more lately. Conversations ended limply because Stacey knew her grandmother couldn't follow them but was too afraid to let her know.

"How's your sandwich?" she asked, changing the subject.

"Hmm, a little dry but it's okay."

"I think I'll have a sandwich too," Stacey replied.

"Stacey…" her grandmother started.

"Yeah?"

Tina looked at her for a few long seconds and then shook her head, "I can't remember."

Stacey forced herself to smile, "That's okay."

Tina looked back down at her food and Stacey fought off the sadness that rose inside of her.

"Anyplace at all, seriously," Stacey said to Amanda the next day.

Amanda yanked her hair up in a ponytail, "I'll text some of my friends. They might know of an office place hiring."

"I just need an interview," Stacey pleaded. "I know I can land the job if they interview me. I'm really good at interviews."

It was true. Where most people got nervous at interviews and proceeded to panic, Stacey had always found herself good at them. Since accepting the job at the 50's diner, she had been offered three other waitressing positions. None of them were better than the job she had.

"You're lucky. I'm dreadful at them. I just sit there like an idiot and sometimes ramble. I never know who they want."

"They just want you to be your best self," Stacey replied.

Amanda rolled her eyes, "That's so corny, Stacey."

She laughed, "Yeah, I guess so."

"I'll put my feelers out. You should ask your other friends, too, just in case."

Stacey watched Amanda leave the break room. There had been an actual lunch rush today when Stacey had come into work. Amanda had been handling it swiftly herself, but Stacey knew back-up was appreciated. Stacey quickly put her things away and headed into the dining room.

At Amanda's suggestion of asking around for an office job, Stacey's mind flicked to Charlie. She didn't want to ask him for any help, even in directing her to a job. The last thing she wanted him to think was that she was seeing him for his money. It felt wrong to even entertain the idea of going to Charlie for help like that.

Even so, he would be the one to know, wouldn't he? If she made it clear she didn't want money from him, then maybe he could help her snag an interview.

She was still mentally debating this as she went over to a patron in one of the booths. Stacey was so caught up in her own thoughts that she didn't realize who it was until the person looked up at her.

It was Adele. Stacey's breath caught. What was it with everyone in her life popping up at her work?

"May I get you something to drink?" Stacey asked primly as if she had no idea who she was.

Adele looked down at the menu and wrinkled her nose, "Coffee. Lots of cream and sugar, please, I suppose. To give it flavor."

Stacey ignored the dig and scribbled it down on her pad. She snuck a glance at Adele, who was staring at the menu. Today, Adele was wearing a light pink blouse that ended perfectly at her wrists, where a bracelet glittering with rubies dangled. The ring around her finger was the engagement ring Stacey had seen yesterday. Adele's hair was up in an elegant bun. Her make-up was flawless, as usual.

Stacey tore her eyes away from Adele. It was pointless to keep comparing their two appearances. Charlie had chosen Stacey, hadn't he? Even if Stacey felt as if she was double Adele's size and was wearing her stupid work uniform, Charlie had still wanted to be with her. At least that's what last night meant, right?

Stacey turned around to get the coffee. She came back a minute later, pouring it out in front of Adele who watched as if pouring coffee was a circus act.

"Do you know what you would like to order?" Stacey asked.

Adele drummed her fingers against the table, "You know, I didn't get it at first. Why Charlie would be interested in you and have no passing interest in me. But I'm starting to understand."

"So, more time on the menu then?" Stacey replied, pretending not to hear Adele.

But that didn't deter Adele from continuing, "Yes, I get it now. At least I think I do. See, Charlie has always seemingly detested the wealth he has. He didn't even want control of the company but the board voted him in after his father had the stroke."

Something must have flickered across Stacey's face because Adele smirked. Her grin looked faintly like a shark's mouth, getting ready to take a bite of its prey.

"Oh, he hadn't told you about the stroke? Yes, his father had a stroke and was basically removed from controlling the company. Sad. So, Charlie was voted in even though Eric wanted it." She shrugged. "This is probably going over your head though."

"I have other tables to tend to, Miss," Stacey said, trying to keep her voice even. "I'll be back in a few minutes."

"Before you go… Stacey, is it? Before you go, Stacey, just remember that you're a passing fancy to Charlie. He always liked to fool around with girls who live so differently than he does. I suppose he finds it interesting. The life he could have had if only, if only. But he will tire of you. He always does. And then he will return to me."

Adele turned back to the menu as Stacey walked away. Her heart was racing. If she hadn't been at work, she would have told Adele off—and then what? As she blindly rounded the corner to the hallway near the kitchen, she felt acutely aware of how out of her depth she truly was.

What was it Adele had said? *Then he will return to me*. Return, as if he had been hers at one point. Charlie hadn't ever said he had been with her—but he hadn't said that he hadn't either.

When Stacey went back onto the main floor, Adele was gone. There was a five-dollar bill thrown onto the table, apparently for the coffee. It was clear she had come just to harass Stacey and nothing more.

Chapter Four

Stacey stepped into Charlie's penthouse, feeling uncomfortable. She was half-expecting Adele to be waiting by the elevator doors, holding a baseball bat firmly in her manicured hands.

Adele wasn't there, of course. It was just Stacey letting her dark mood get the best of her. She knew what she had to do. She was just dreading it.

"That you, Stacey?" Charlie's voice came from the living room.

"Yeah, it's me," she said, forcing herself to walk down the hallway.

To her surprise, Tony was here. He was on the balcony, talking on his phone. She could see just his back, slightly hunched over as he discussed something. Charlie was sitting on the couch with his tablet in his lap. He had a beer on the table next to him. His tie was undone and hanging loosely around his neck. Stacey felt her heart constrict at the sight of him.

"I didn't know Tony was here," she said casually.

Charlie looked over at him, "Yeah, he came by to discuss a few things. Nothing important. He just wants to avoid his girlfriend."

"Why?" she asked, sitting down next to Charlie.

"He wants to break up with her but keeps stalling. Funny how he's so great with business but when it comes to personal relationships, he turns into a little boy."

Stacey's gaze flicked back up to Tony. He had turned around now although he hadn't seen her. He was handsome but in a different way than Charlie. Charlie always looked as if he was in on a joke no one else knew about. He had those puppy dog eyes and a smile that lit up the room. Tony was handsome in a colder way. Even on the yacht, his smile and flirting felt as if it was something he did more out of habit than with meaning.

"How was your day?" Charlie asked her.

She tore her gaze away from Tony and back to him, "Okay. Actually, I need to talk to—"

It was then that Tony came inside. When he saw Stacey, he smiled at her but it didn't reach his eyes.

"Everything okay?" Charlie asked.

"That wasn't Kate, if that is what you were asking."

Stacey guessed that was the name of his girlfriend. She remembered her from the boat, pretty and gorgeous and determined to get his attention.

Tony continued, "Just an issue at the office downtown."

"What's wrong?" Charlie's eyebrows furrowed as if Tony's problem was Charlie's problem as well.

"Had a few people quit, that's all. They wanted a pay raise and it had been turned down. Now we're short staffed."

Stacey's head snapped up at this. Before Charlie could even reply, she asked, "What sort of positions are open?"

Tony looked at her closely for a second or two before replying, "Couple of financial advisors and a receptionist position."

"What about me? For the receptionist position, obviously, not the financial ones," she was rambling again but was determined to get her message across. "You can interview me. I'm not just asking for the job."

Charlie and Tony exchanged glances. Finally, he nodded.

"Sure. Give me your contact information and I'll have someone call you to set it up."

Relief swept through her. "Amazing. Thank you so much," she said and rattled off her phone number to Tony.

He finished typing it into his phone and then nodded at her. "Alright, well, I have to go. Wish me luck." He directed this to Charlie as he left.

Stacey watched him go. As the elevator doors shut, she was aware that she was alone with Charlie now.

Her nerves returned hard and fast as Charlie pulled her in for a kiss.

If our lips touch, my nerve will crumble, Stacey thought and turned her head sharply to the side. His lips grazed her cheek.

"Hey, I need to talk to you," she said.

He pulled away from her, "What's wrong?"

"Adele stopped by at work today."

Anger clouded Charlie's features briefly before he ran his fingers through his hair. "Did she really?"

"Yeah. Just to sort of…ward me away from you, I guess."

"I thought I made it perfectly clear to her that whatever she planned with my father doesn't mean anything to me," he grumbled.

Stacey wanted to tell him Adele was confident that whatever he thought didn't matter. But repeating what she had said about Charlie liking girls in *different worlds* stung too much.

Instead, she decided to plow through what she had come to say. "I don't know if this will work, Charlie. You know, between you and me. I want it too. I really do. But having your fiancée threaten me at work because I'm seeing you is a little too much. Not to mention I'd be dealing with whatever your family might throw my way. And maybe, just maybe, it wouldn't affect you too much. No matter what happens, you'd be okay in the end. But I might not. If anyone were to get hurt in this situation, it would be me. And it just isn't healthy for me to keep trying to push these feelings aside. If I'm feeling overwhelmed now, what will it turn into later?"

She had said this all in one burst without pausing to let Charlie speak. But she stopped speaking as if all the words had been emptied out onto a pile on the floor by his feet. He stared at her with a strange expression on his face. Stacey couldn't read it. She wasn't good at breaking up with people. When she had caught Jake cheating on her, it was a declaration. A clean break.

This was different. She was breaking up with Charlie because their worlds were too different. She wasn't sure if she could handle living in his.

Finally, Charlie found his voice, "So…that's it then?"

"Do you understand? I'd rather leave now before the situation is even more over my head. Your family wouldn't want us to be together. I can't have Adele suddenly pop up in places just to threaten me to leave you. I have too many other things going on to worry about a crazed stalker."

Charlie cleared his throat and said softly, "I understand."

She was disarmed by this. She had been expecting anger. Maybe some sort of passionate speech about why they should keep trying. But Charlie just looked resigned. Stacey didn't know what else to say. She got to her feet.

"Bye, Charlie," Stacey said awkwardly.

Charlie didn't respond. She turned away and quickly walked down the hallway toward the elevators. As she reached for the elevator button, she paused. *Is this it?* She had been expecting more. She thought he would come after her, that he would have tried to stop her.

She pressed the button. Tears sprung to her eyes as the elevator arrived to take her down, away from Charlie.

"Did you hear me?"

"No, sorry. What?"

Allison rolled her eyes, "What is up with you today? You're so out of it."

Stacey looked up from the store window she had been staring into. It was her day off, three days since she broke up with Charlie. There hadn't been a peep from him. Even though she was the one who had broken up with him to save her from more heartache, she couldn't understand how he hadn't reached out at least once.

"Sorry," Stacey said lamely.

Allison had dragged her out to window shop with Tina. Stacey had agreed because she thought it would be good to get out of the house. If she had let herself dwell on her situation, she would have spent the entire day in bed.

But it seemed she wasn't very good at focusing. Her sister stared at her, waiting for her to explain herself.

"I have a headache," she said, trying to look convincing.

"Sure," Allison said with a snort and walked away, catching up to Tina, who had wandered further ahead.

Stacey watched her sister. The annoyance she felt being around Allison lately had faded. Her mind was focused on Charlie instead. Even though she felt so sure she was doing the right thing, she couldn't help but wonder if she was making a mistake.

Maybe Stacey should have dealt with his family and Adele head on. Was it wrong of her to have jumped ship so early? She pushed the thoughts out of her mind. There was no point in dwelling on them. She had made her choice. Charlie's life was too chaotic for her. It was filled with drama and uncertainty. Stacey had her own issues to deal with.

She wandered up to where Tina and Allison were looking at a store window. Allison looked over her shoulder. "I don't know why you're so distracted today. Don't you have that interview tomorrow?"

It was true, she did. Tony's local office had called this morning to schedule a meeting. She set it up, but even that made her feel guilty. She had leapt at the chance to get that interview, breaking up with Charlie not five minutes later. Surely that had to look bad.

"Yeah, I do."

"You'll do great," Tina said, heading into the shop.

The two sisters followed their grandmother into the store. It was filled with mostly tourist trinkets. Tina stopped at the snow globes to admire them. Allison glanced over at Stacey.

"So, you gonna tell me?"

"Tell you what?"

"Who you fucked the other day."

"Jesus! Keep your voice down," Stacey snapped. "Why are you so crass?"

"Because it makes you upset," Allison said, laughing.

Stacey turned away from her, pretending to be interested in a row of ugly jewelry boxes. But Allison didn't get the hint and hovered over her shoulder.

"It doesn't matter," Stacey finally relented. "We broke up."

"Oh. Sorry about that, sis. Whatever, he was a jerk to begin with. You sorta suck at picking them." Allison saw the look on her sister's face and quickly added, "No offense."

Stacey didn't reply. Instead, she looked over to make sure Tina was alright. She had picked up another snow globe and was shaking it. There was something slightly glassy in her grandmother's eyes that sent a pain through her heart.

Behind her, however, Allison was determined to keep the conversation going, "Jake was alright at first, I guess. I really thought you two might work out. You know, when I saw him recently at the deli, he said he was single."

Stacey whirled around, "Are you suggesting I get back with him?"

Her sister shrugged.

"How can you suggest that? After what he did to me?"

"Fine, fine, forget I even mentioned him." She held her hands up as if to ward Stacey off, "Listen, if the new guy didn't like how you looked, forget him."

She stared at Allison who seemed oblivious to what she had just said. She crossed her arms.

"Why can't I have been the one to break up with this guy? Why do you assume it was him? And why do you assume it was because of how I look?"

"Well, I just know in the past how guys have treated you. Are you angry that I just assumed you were dumped? I swear, you just look for a reason to be pissed off."

"No, I don't. And I broke up with him."

The two stared at each other as if they were each deciding how much they wanted to bicker in the store. But Stacey was tired and worn out. She didn't feel like fighting with Allison again.

Instead, she turned around and went to check on Tina.

Chapter Five

Tony seemed to own a lot of different businesses like Charlie did. Charlie focused on construction and investing whereas Tony focused more on the media and publicity for celebrities.

The office in the city where Stacey had her interview was one of the media branches. They owned a local news station and had a slew of celebrities that used them for publicity.

As she waited for her interview to start, Stacey tried to quell her nerves. This job was something she knew she could do. The woman who had called her to set up the interview had made it clear that the position entailed tasks such as making copies, scheduling appointments and events, and keeping the front desk running smoothly alongside two other receptionists. Tony was willing to take a chance on her by getting her an interview. Stacey didn't want to blow it.

She still felt as if she was walking around in a fog. She hadn't been expecting to miss Charlie so much. She also hadn't been expecting how much she hoped he would have reached out to her. Why? Stacey asked herself for the millionth time. Even if he had called, what could she say? She couldn't have gone back to him.

Stacey pushed thoughts of Charlie out of her mind and looked around the waiting room. There was no one else in sight. The TV was playing the news. Everything was decorated in bright colors and there were paintings on the walls. It would have been cozy if she hadn't felt so nervous.

In front of her was the desk she would be working behind if she were hired. A woman sat behind the counter, typing rapidly on the computer. Stacey blanched at the idea of being asked about computers. She had never owned one. All she knew how to do she had learned at the library.

After about ten minutes of waiting, one of the side doors opened, and a smartly dressed woman came out. She introduced herself as Ms. Stark and escorted Stacey down the hallway. It was decorated more of the same. She didn't see anyone else. The area was quiet although in the distance she could hear music.

Ms. Stark opened another door. They entered a small meeting room with a table and chairs. Stacey sat down across the other side of the table and tried to wash everything else from her mind.

It was time to show her best self.

Thirty minutes later, Stacey was shown around the rest of the establishment. The job wasn't offered to her then but she couldn't help but feel confident. She doubted they took time to show every person who interviewed a quick tour of the office.

As Stacey was being shown one of the meeting rooms, someone stepped out of the elevator nearby.

It was Tony. Stacey bit her tongue to stop herself from calling out to him. She would hate it to look as if they were chummy.

He was dressed as formally as she had ever seen him. His hair was slicked back, and he was speaking rapidly into his cell phone, in Chinese, or more specifically, Mandarin, as she found out from Tony later. Stacey didn't understand a word. He finished up the call and turned around.

"Stacey?"

For some reason, she felt a blush rise on her face. Ms. Stark started talking in her high-pitched voice to Tony about how Stacey was here for an interview.

"Yes, I know who Stacey is. Are you showing her around?" he asked with a smile.

"Yes, we were just about to—"

"I'll take it from here," he said, gently interrupting Ms. Stark.

The look that the woman gave Stacey was all she needed to know that this was unusual. Ms. Stark nodded and walked off, looking back one last time at the two of them.

Stacey, feeling nervous and slightly uncomfortable, said, "You don't have to do this."

"Of course, I do," he replied, still smiling. "Ms. Stark is a fantastic worker but can be a bit too bubbly."

"Yes, well, that is one way of putting it," Stacey replied lightly.

Tony let out a laugh. There was something comforting about it that she couldn't put her finger on. As he showed her the rest of the company offices, she found herself relaxing. It hardly felt like a job interview now.

"I have an office here, too, although I'm not here often," he said as they walked down the hallway on the second floor.

He stopped at the door at the end of the hallway and unlocked it. They stepped inside. It was a simple office. For some reason, Stacey had been expecting something completely over the top. She had been thinking about his yacht. She had assumed if he owned a yacht, everything would be grand like that.

But his office was clean and simply decorated. Even the view was subpar—just the street and the buildings across from it. There was nothing to set it apart from any other office Stacey had already seen.

"Nothing much. Like I said, I'm not here often. But I try to have an office set up in each of my buildings."

"Where do you spend most of your time?"

"Around. All over. I have offices here and in China so I bounce between the two," Tony replied.

Stacey looked at one of the paintings. It was an ocean spreading out as far as she could see. In the middle rose a dragon.

"You like that? Don't be fooled. I try to fill my office with at least one token Chinese-looking piece of art. People seem to expect it. Do you want some coffee?"

Stacey looked over her shoulder, "Oh, sure. Thanks." She looked back at the painting. "You mean you don't like this?"

"Nah. I think I got it at a garage sale."

"People really expect Chinese things because you're Chinese?" Stacey asked him as he handed her a cup of coffee.

"Of course," he said laughing. "Might as well give them what they want."

"Well, thank you again for allowing me to come in for an interview. I really appreciate it even if I don't get the job."

"Ms. Stark doesn't show people around the office unless she is impressed. I wouldn't be too worried. Although you look worried."

"Do I?"

"Yeah. Worried about the job?"

Worried about everything, Stacey wanted to blurt out but instead said, "Just a lot going on."

Tony nodded. A ring on his thumb flashed. It was gold with a giant emerald in the center. It glimmered under the office lights.

"My dad gave me this," he said, having noticed Stacey looking at it. "When I was little. It used to be too large for me to wear, so I hid it under my pillow every night as a good luck charm."

"Did it bring you good luck?" Stacey asked.

"Not at first," Tony replied and there was something a little sad in his tone that brought her up short.

Silence fell between them. Her brain tried to find something to fill the silence with, but it was Tony who spoke first.

"Anyway, I'm glad that you will be working here. It'll be nice to see a friendly face every day. And at events as well, since I suppose Charlie will be taking you out."

At the mention of Charlie, Stacey balked. She looked away from Tony. Something must have shown on her face because he raised his eyebrows.

Seeing no point in hiding it or wanting to make him think she was keeping secrets, Stacey said, "I broke up with him. A couple of days ago. That day you were at his place actually."

Surprise crossed Tony's eyes followed by something else that she couldn't make out. Then he said, "I didn't know. I'm sorry to have brought it up."

"No, I should have said something." She looked down at her coffee. "I hope you don't think—I wouldn't want you to think that I—I mean, if you decide to offer me the job, I wouldn't want you to have offered it to me because of Charlie. So, it's better you know."

Tony's gaze softened. "I wouldn't offer you a job based solely on him or any connection. I actually broke up with my girlfriend the same day you broke up with Charlie."

"Oh! Charlie mentioned you two…" She made a gesture with her hands as if to signal that Tony and his girlfriend were on the rocks.

He smiled a little, but his eyes told a different story. "She wanted more of me and I couldn't give it to her. I'm not ready to settle down. I didn't want to keep her hanging around thinking I would change my mind. Better to end it. She was upset but it will be better for her in the long run."

"You didn't want to settle down with her?"

"It wasn't anything personal," Tony replied. "I'm just not ready for that and she was."

For the first time since she had met Tony, Stacey saw a real person beneath the business glamor. It was strange but endearing to see someone struggle with regular problems. Unlike when she met Charlie, she knew Tony was a billionaire. She had assumed everything would be perfect in his world. But he looked upset at the mention of his break-up.

It was this sudden vulnerability that spurned Stacey to ask her next question, "What is up with Charlie and Adele?"

At the mention of Adele, Tony's eyebrows shot up. He took a sip of his coffee before giving a proper response.

Finally, he asked, "You met Adele?"

"Three times, technically."

"And you're still standing here. Amazing."

"You don't like her?" Stacey inquired.

"What's to like?" Tony remarked as he turned around to head toward his desk. "You've met her."

"She came to see me at work." Stacey paused for a moment, searching for the right way to word things. "She said that Charlie dates girls like me for fun. That'd it be a passing fancy. He would eventually go back to her."

"I've known Charlie for quite some time and I can tell you he never liked Adele in that way. She's liked him for years. When his father came up with this stupid idea, Adele jumped right on it. She thought she would win him over right away, see? That Charlie would leap at the chance to marry her."

"No such luck?"

"No. He didn't have a good relationship with his father or his brother. So being shoved into some marriage with Adele just rubbed him the wrong way. Even if he did care for her at some point, that has long since died." He paused. "Why? Were you worried he would leave you for her?"

Stacey decided since Tony had confided in her about his own relationship that she could at least do the same. "No. No, it was partly because of Adele. Mostly it was just the fact that I felt in over my head. See, I didn't know who he was when we started dating. So, finding out and then having some woman threatening me—it was just too much. Especially with everything going on like—"

She cut herself off and shook her head. "Geez, sorry. What am I doing just rambling to you like this?"

"I don't mind," Tony said with warmth in his voice. "Really. I talk about business so often. Sometimes I forget there're other things going on in the world as well."

"My grandmother is sick. She probably needs a nurse or to be placed in a home. But money is really tight and my sister is useless for help so—" she said, trailing off with a shrug. "Worrying about that and finding a new job and then all of Charlie's stuff. Maybe I'm selfish but I just had to put myself first."

Tony was studying her. There was something different in his gaze that made her want to look away. But she didn't. Instead, she met his stare. Her heart skipped a beat.

"I'm truly sorry about your grandmother," he finally said in a soft voice. "Struggling with a sick family member—it isn't easy on anyone."

Stacey was going to ask if he was speaking from experience, but his phone rang. He pulled it from his pocket and looked down at the screen.

"I should take this. I'll have Ms. Stark escort you out."

Stacey felt her stomach lurch. She was disappointed the conversation ended so abruptly. The thought came to her quickly and surprised her.

Tony smiled gently at her as his phone kept ringing. "It was lovely talking to you, Stacey."

Chapter Six

Stacey dreamed she was back at her parents' house. The lights were on and the TV was blaring the news. She stood in the kitchen. Everything was how she had left it the day her parents died. The fridge was covered with Allison's drawings and Stacey's tests demonstrating excellence.

She looked down at herself. She was not a child, not any longer. She looked around the kitchen and then slowly moved toward the living room. It felt as if she was walking underwater. Her limbs weighed a thousand pounds each as she tried to move into the living room.

When she finally stepped inside, the TV turned to static. The sudden noise made her wince. She walked over to mute it. Her parents would be furious if they knew she left all the lights on as well as the TV. What was she thinking?

Stacey turned off the TV and turned around. On the couch was Charlie. His sudden appearance startled her, but she felt rooted to the spot. He stood up and languidly walked over to her. He didn't seem to be affected by the quicksand that surrounded Stacey's own limbs.

He dragged one finger down the side of her face and tilted her chin up to meet her eyes. Her heart beat so rapidly she thought she might faint. She wanted to tell him she missed him. She wanted to ask him why he was there, in her childhood home.

But none of that occurred. Around the corner came Adele. She wore a snake around her neck as she glided toward Charlie. Stacey tried to pull Charlie toward her but Adele wrapped her hands around his waist and pulled him away.

Stacey couldn't do anything. All she could do was watch Adele pull him away from her. Her feet refused to move. She wanted to pull him back—tell him she missed him—

Suddenly, Stacey's eyes snapped open. A strange noise filled her head. It took her a few moments to realize it was her phone ringing. She wiped her eyes, trying to erase the dream that clung to her, as she picked up.

By the time she grabbed her phone, it had stopped ringing. The voicemail icon appeared a moment later. Stacey listened to it. The fog of the dream instantly vanished when she heard the message.

I got the job, she thought to herself, replaying the message from Ms. Stark just to make sure she had heard it correctly. She couldn't believe it. The money she would be getting from the job would make things a lot easier on her. She would be able to afford care for Tina and pay the bills with a little extra to spare.

Her head was swimming. Even though she had gone to the interview and was confident she performed well, she hadn't quite expected to land the job.

She sat up in bed. She was working an evening shift at the restaurant tonight and lay down to take a quick nap before getting ready. The dream quickly forgotten, Stacey got out of bed to tell Allison and Tina the good news.

Yet when she walked out into the living room, Allison was sitting on the couch crying into Tina's lap.

"What's going on?"

Allison looked up. Her eyes were rimmed with red and her cheeks puffy. For a brief second, Stacey thought maybe something truly bad had happened.

But then her sister wailed, "Jacob dumped me!"

She broke into fresh tears. Stacey's first thought was that they were never going to get the bracelet back now. Her second was that she was pretty sure her sister didn't care at all about Jacob. He had been boring and clearly only into himself. What her sister was mourning was the loss of yet another chance at landing a man with tons of money.

"Sorry for your loss," Stacey replied, hoping she sounded as if she meant it.

Allison kept crying and shook her head. "I think he met someone in Europe! He called me and said things wouldn't work out. He said we were just too different!"

"Ah, dear," Tina murmured, stroking Allison's hair.

Stacey fought not to roll her eyes. Anytime Allison ended up single, even if she was the one who did the breaking up, she acted as if it was the end of the world. Stacey, who had been looking forward to sharing her good fortune with Allison and Tina, saw it fade in front of her eyes.

"I didn't realize you cared so much about him," she quipped.

Allison scowled, "Don't be a bitch now."

"Allison!" Tina scolded.

"But it's true! She's just upset because she got dumped, too."

She was trying to goad Stacey into a fight but Stacey was too happy about the job to care. All Stacey said was, "I dumped him," and headed toward the kitchen.

She could hear Tina comforting Allison in the living room. Even with her sister dealing with the break-up and losing the bracelet forever, it couldn't spoil the fact that Stacey had landed the receptionist job.

As she rummaged through the cupboard for something to eat, finally settling on some instant noodles, her sister came in.

"You want some?" Stacey offered, pulling out another pack.

"No." Allison sniffed.

"Alright."

"You don't seem bothered."

"About what?"

"Well, I can't get the bracelet back now."

"Yup," Stacey replied. "Oh well."

Allison narrowed her eyes. "I thought for sure you'd flip your shit."

"I considered that thing lost as soon as you gave it back to him with your lame-ass romantic gesture," Stacey admitted. "Besides, I got the job that I interviewed for. While the money we could have gotten for that bracelet would have been useful, at least I'll have more income."

"Oh. Well, congrats," Allison mumbled.

"Don't worry. I won't let that steal your thunder of another billionaire breaking your heart. You're on a bad run, aren't you?" Stacey said as she filled a pot with water.

"Don't be such a bitch."

"Well, I guess that means you'll be crashing here a bit longer, right?"

Allison at least looked abashed at this, "Uh, yeah, well, I guess."

"It's fine. You can stay," she replied as she put the pot on the stove.

"Thanks. Sorry for, uh, calling you a bitch."

"It's fine. Wouldn't expect things to change suddenly."

She could tell Allison was biting her tongue. She knew her sister well enough to know that she was pissed off Jacob dumped her. She wanted to argue with someone but also needed a place to stay. That meant she couldn't keep digging in like she was. Stacey had to admit she was enjoying this a bit.

"Well, maybe next time will be the one, right? Surely, all these years of effort have to pay off sometime."

Allison frowned and opened her mouth before quickly closing it. Stacey watched her sister leave the kitchen, clearly hoping to find sympathy from Tina instead of her.

The next week was a complete blur. Stacey began training at Tony's office during the day and covering shifts at the restaurant during the evenings. By the time she got home, she was so exhausted that she fell asleep in a matter of seconds.

Things became even faster-paced as she entered her second week. This was going to be the week that she was released into the office without training wheels. Stacey had been relieved to see herself picking up on things quickly, even the computer. All the hours she had spent on the library's computers had ended up helping her out. She was a fast learner.

Stacey hadn't seen Tony since her interview day. She had been thinking about him, on and off, as she was learning the ropes of her new job. Everyone at the office spoke highly of him, which Stacey knew was unusual. Everyone seemed to genuinely like him, and they appreciated him working in an office that didn't show off his billionaire status.

On the first day of her second week, a summer storm ripped through the city. It had been ages since it had rained this hard and Stacey found herself making sure everything was okay at home before heading out to work.

Allison had been claiming she was too depressed to do anything around the apartment. Stacey decided that once she had figured out the best way to get her grandmother professional care, she would force Allison to get a job. She was sick of letting her sister crash at her home and not do anything because she was too busy sulking in her misery.

The storm started early in the morning. By mid-afternoon, the rain was coming down in thick sheets, blanketing the city. It was shortly after the power flickered on and off the first time that Tony stopped into the office.

Stacey hadn't been expecting him. It wasn't as if she was kept in the loop about when he would be arriving. She had been focused on trying to get her computer to connect to the internet which kept going down due to the storm.

She heard him before she saw him and looked over her computer monitor. Tony was speaking to Ms. Stark in a low voice about something. She was nodding a lot and looked like a bobble head. Stacey had noticed in the short time working there that Ms. Stark always seemed to be overly caffeinated, reminding her of Amanda from the restaurant.

Tony looked up over Ms. Stark's head. His eyes settled on Stacey, who ducked behind the computer screen. She felt embarrassed. She didn't want him to get the impression that she had been staring at him. She was determined to not look at him again and threw herself into work when suddenly the power went out completely.

The office was plunged into total darkness. It was already dark outside, so windows offered no extra light. The rain thumped loudly against the building along with a wind that had come along with the storm. It had been a while since a summer storm this intense had rolled through.

A few people began to mumble about why the generator wasn't coming back on. Of course, an office like this would have a back-up generator. She could hear Ms. Stark asking someone else about why the generator wasn't on.

"Something fascinating on the screen?"

Stacey looked up and was staring directly into Tony's eyes. Her heart skipped a beat, and she shook her head.

"No, just waiting for the power to come back on."

"Generator needs to be reset. I'm going down to check it. Want to come with me?"

"Me?" Stacey asked curiously.

Tony shrugged, "That way you'll know for next time."

"Oh, um, sure," Stacey replied shyly.

As Tony turned around to tell Ms. Stark he was going to reset the generator, Stacey couldn't help but find his excuse lacking. In the back of her mind, she knew that Tony wanted to get her alone. The couple of times he had flirted with her was not lost on her.

There's no way, she thought to herself. There could be no way that he was interested in her like that, no way that Stacey was interested in him like that. She had been sucked into Charlie's life once. She wasn't going to flirt with another billionaire.

"Come on," Tony said to her over his shoulder.

She got to her feet and tried to ignore Ms. Stark, staring at her. No one else noticed, nor cared that she was going down to reset the generator with Tony. They walked through the hallway toward the basement which he unlocked with a key. A dark staircase led downstairs.

"Creepy," Stacey remarked. "Isn't this how horror movies start?"

Tony laughed and pulled out his phone, turning on a flashlight app. Then he led the way down the stairs first. Stacey followed. She was slower than he was because she was in heels, but Tony waited for her every few steps.

The basement was filled with a random assortment of things. The musty smell of old paper and boxes tickled her nose. Dust filled the air, and she fought the urge to sneeze. Tony looked around the room.

"We probably need to clean this place out at some point."

"At least dust it."

There was a sudden boom of thunder that caused Stacey to make a startled noise. Tony was by her side right away as if she was in some sort of real danger. She felt embarrassed by her reaction.

"Are you okay?"

"Yeah, sorry," she said. "Just wasn't expecting it to be so loud."

This close to Tony, Stacey could feel how warm he was. His cologne was different from what Charlie usually wore. It was deeper and spicier. There was something comforting about it.

"This way." He led her to another door at the back of the basement.

Another clap of thunder rumbled out but Stacey didn't jump this time. She refused to let herself look like a baby again. It was just a storm. Tony stopped in front of the door and opened it. The hinges creaked loudly. Stacey half expected some monster to leap out at them.

Instead, it looked as if this was where the breakers for the building were. Tony stepped inside, holding up his phone to illuminate the wall.

"Internet, power, security, all of that comes down here. The generator is here as well. We haven't had to use it in a while so it just needs to be reset. It'll be good for you to know in case Ms. Stark isn't available."

Stacey couldn't imagine a time when Ms. Stark wouldn't be in the office but didn't say that. She nodded but realized it was dark down here and he couldn't see her.

"Okay," she said aloud.

She followed him to the generator as he held his phone up to illuminate it. He opened a panel to expose several buttons inside.

"Would you please turn on your flashlight app too?"

"Well, no. My phone doesn't run apps."

This seemed to startle Tony. He turned his head to look at her. The look on his face was comical only because he was surprised by something so small.

"I just have a flip phone. I don't even have it on me. I keep it in my purse during the day," she explained.

"Wow," he finally said as another boom of thunder sounded out. "Sorry, I just assumed…"

"It's okay. I get it. Almost everyone has a smartphone now."

"Well, come look at this, at least."

The spot in front of the generator panel was a tight fit for the two of them. But Stacey managed to slide into the small space as best as she could. Her side was mushed against Tony's side. The sudden closeness to him made every nerve of her body snap to attention.

"You just have to turn it off all the way. Sometimes this thing is weird and thinks it is off but it isn't. So, pressing this," he said as he pressed a red button, "will power it off completely. Then we wait a full minute."

"Okay," she murmured, suddenly feeling very shy.

As they waited, he tilted his face to look at hers. They were incredibly close. Their noses could touch if she only leaned forward a little.

"Settling in here okay?" Tony asked her softly.

"Yeah. Everyone has been nice. I can't thank you enough for the job."

"You earned it. Apparently, you gave the best interview so you got the job."

"Right, but…" She hesitated before speaking. "I had no previous office experience."

"I was willing to take a chance on you," Tony said gently.

Something in his tone, the warmth perhaps, made Stacey blush. She could hear her heart beating. Being this close to him had Stacey wondering if he could hear it as well. It would be embarrassing if he knew what an odd reaction she was having because he was so near.

"Well, thank you," she finally said.

"How are you holding up? With the break-up?"

Stacey was surprised at the sudden mention of Charlie. Yet his eyes betrayed nothing. In this low lighting, it was impossible to see what Tony was thinking.

"I'm okay. I mean, I'm the one who ended it, so why dwell on the past?" She cleared her throat. "What about you?"

"Ah, well, I'm okay. Like you said, I wanted to end it. So why dwell on it?" he said softly.

Being this close to him, speaking of past relationships, made Stacey forget that she was down here in this basement with Tony. It even made her forget that Tony was like Charlie—rich and well off, part of another world completely. They were just two people who had ended things because of the cards life had dealt them.

Stacey was going to open her mouth to ask something else when suddenly the power flicked on. The sudden burst of light in the basement startled her. She gasped in surprise and closed her eyes for a couple of seconds.

Tony cleared his throat loudly. "Power is back. Well, I'll tell you anyway. After you wait a minute, press this green button and it resets the generator."

He pressed it hastily, and the generator made a beeping noise. The screen flickered and a green light flashed indicating it was ready. Stacey wriggled her way out of the tight space. Her mouth felt dry. The sudden blast of the lights made her feel as if she had been on stage and the spotlight had found her. Whatever the strange spell was that had settled over the two of them, it had quickly dissipated.

"We should go back up now," Tony said, ending the discussion about their recent breakups.

Chapter Seven

"Can you repeat that, dear?" her grandmother asked after Stacey had recounted the story about the power going off at work.

"Which part?"

Tina scrunched up her face as if trying to remember before saying, "What were we talking about?"

"The weather," Stacey said, sighing inwardly.

It wasn't even that she had told her grandmother the story. It was that telling her the story and having her forget it almost immediately made her heart break.

"It's been raining all day," her grandmother said, looking out the window.

"Yeah, it's going to be raining all week, I guess," Stacey replied. "Things may be sort of crazy. But we'll be okay."

Tina turned to look at Stacey and asked, "Whatever happened to those men who wanted us to leave?"

At the mention of Charlie and his company, a stab of guilt bloomed over Stacey's chest and she replied, "They lost interest. So, we don't have to move."

Relief swept across Tina's face, "Oh, good. I would have hated to move somewhere else."

"Me too," Stacey said, turning around to hide her face.

It wasn't easy to forget Charlie. Even though she told herself that she didn't owe Charlie anything and had to put herself first, it was hard to remember that. He had switched around so much to date her. She wasn't sure how to appease the guilt that seemed to lodge itself in her gut when she thought about it for too long.

The front door slammed, signalling that Allison had returned from whatever crazy venture she was up to today. At least she had left the house instead of moping around about that wet-reed Jacob for another day.

"It's raining so fucking much," she heard Allison grumble.

"Language," Tina remarked as she came into the dining room.

"Sorry, sorry," Allison said. "Man, it's cold in here."

Stacey looked over her shoulder. Allison was dressed in a black t-shirt that was a size too small. It clung to her wetly and hugged her curves. Her jeans were also wet, which must have been uncomfortable.

"Dear, you are soaking wet," Tina observed. "Go change out of those things and put on some dry clothes."

"Yeah, I think I will. Thanks."

Stacey, knowing her sister better than anyone, followed her to the hallway. She had shoved some clothes in Tina's chest of drawers and was rummaging through them. Stacey leaned against the doorframe.

"Nice day?"

"I was trying the puppy dog act with Jacob."

"What, soaking wet clothes, staring at him outside his hotel?"

Allison pulled out a fresh t-shirt. "Something like that."

"Any luck?"

"A little. I pretended I was meeting someone else there at the diner across the street. Timed it so we would run into each other."

"Geez, Allison, is it really worth this much effort? The guy is a total tool."

"Yeah, yeah, I know. But the money, Stacey. If I snag him, imagine the wealth. Not just for me. All of us."

Allison moved past her and headed toward the bathroom to change. Stacey watched her sister and shook her head. She still didn't understand how Allison could put so much energy toward these types of men. Surely, she would grow out of it? She would see how silly it was to try to snag someone rich just to pay her way through life.

The bathroom door shut and locked. Whatever Stacey had been thinking, she knew it was pointless to try to bring it up with Allison. Better to choose her battles.

The storm continued through the next day. When Stacey arrived at the office, she found herself looking for Tony. She felt foolish for doing so. The shared moment in the basement the other day had been nothing. She was losing her head over minor things just to try to forget Charlie.

Even so, when she left work that day to cover a shift at the restaurant, she felt disappointed at not having seen him.

"How is the job?" Amanda asked as Stacey headed into the break room to drop her things off.

"Going well. Exhausted though."

"Well, we close soon. Are you still going to take that job at the 50's diner?" Amanda asked as she let her hair out of her ponytail.

"I think so. The extra money would be nice," Stacey replied although she was also thinking it would be a good distraction from how she was feeling about her love life. "You look cute. What's going on with you?"

"I have a date with Brad," she said, wiggling her eyebrows. "He asked me out the other day. Throwing myself at him for ages finally paid off."

"Congrats to you. That means…"

"Yup, you're stuck with Chester as the cook."

Chester was the part-time cook, a grumpy old man that William called in for favors sometimes. Stacey hadn't worked with him in a long time but always detested it. Last time he had pinched her ass, and she almost clocked him.

"Great. Well, good luck on your date," Stacey said, knowing how long Amanda had been harboring a crush on Brad.

"Thanks," she beamed. "Hey, whatever happened to that cute guy that came by to talk to you that day?"

Was everyone keen on mentioning Charlie in some way to her? Stacey tried not to cringe and gave a noncommittal shrug.

"Nothing came of it."

"Ah, that's a shame." She looked at the time on her phone. "I have to go. Have fun dealing with Chester."

Stacey waved goodbye and headed out to deal with the one family in the restaurant. The restaurant was closing next week. It would be strange saying goodbye to a place where she had spent four years working. This place, always intended to be a stepping-stone to better things, had ended up feeling like a different sort of home to her.

She knew working at the other diner would be a lot of work. Even now, she was flat out exhausted when she got home from working both at the office and here. But Stacey felt if she were to stop for even a minute, thoughts that she had been trying to stifle would surface. She didn't want to dwell on Charlie or wonder why she had been let down at not seeing Tony today.

Even though the office job made life a lot easier money-wise, Stacey was still terrified of suddenly having the rug pulled out from under her. The last thing she wanted was something to go wrong at Tony's office without a backup job. She felt as if she had lucked into this one. At any time, it could be snatched away, leaving Stacey grappling for money again.

Even with Chester, her shift went by at a good pace. Customers dropped in non-stop during the night. Most were William's friends visiting for the last time before the diner closed for good.

Stacey was tired when she got home but she was growing used to being exhausted.

When she opened the door to the apartment, Tina was sitting on the couch. She had her knitting needles in her lap again although it appeared as if no project had been started. The TV was showing the weather. They only got a handful of channels because Stacey didn't want to put money toward paying for a pricier cable package. Tina seemed to always have it on the weather channel.

"Hey. Is it still going to rain?" Stacey asked by way of greeting.

Tina nodded, "Looks like it. More big sweeping summer storms are coming our way."

"It's been a while since we had storms this bad," Stacey said as she took off her shoes. "I guess we should get used to them."

Stacey turned to put her bag on the table near the front door. She checked her phone just in case someone had tried to reach her. There were no messages. She turned around to ask her grandmother if she had eaten, and let out a strangled noise of surprise.

In the few seconds that Stacey had spent turning around and checking her phone, Tina's eyes had rolled into the back of her head. She was convulsing on the couch. In the back of Stacey's mind, she knew that her grandmother was having a seizure. But all she could feel was blind panic at seeing Tina in pain.

She returned to her phone, fumbling to dial 911 as she rushed over to Tina. Her grandmother was about to slide off the couch but Stacey managed to grab her. Her arms were rigid and had gone straight above her head. Her feet had banged against the coffee table and were currently kicking as if Tina was being pulled under a current.

"911, please state your emergency?" A proper female sounding voice came over the line.

Stacey gripped her phone and tried to stop Tina from injuring herself more on the table. "My grandmother is having a seizure. She's never had one before!"

The operator tried to talk Stacey through what to do as an ambulance was dispatched. All she could feel was overwhelming fear churning in her stomach as she watched her grandmother shake and rock back and forth for what felt like an eternity.

By the time the paramedics arrived, the seizure had subsided. Tina was on the floor with her head in Stacey's lap as the EMTs came in to treat her.

The next hour was a blur. Tina was loaded into the ambulance while Stacey followed. Her grandmother looked so tiny and frail, strapped in the gurney. Her skin looked as if it was paper-thin. Stacey gripped her grandmother's bony hand and tried to swallow her tears. She didn't want to sob the entire ride to the hospital. She didn't want to be hysterical in front of the paramedics. The tears threatened to spill while she gripped Tina's hand tighter.

Tina was whisked away to be evaluated once they arrived at the hospital. Stacey found herself alone in the waiting room. The hospital was freezing cold. Even now, she could hear the storm beating against the hospital roof. She sat down in one of the uncomfortable chairs and stared down at the floor.

She knew she should be calling her sister. Allison needed to know that Tina had had a seizure and was in the hospital. Her phone was shoved in her pocket. She tried to call Allison, but there was no answer.

"Voicemail is currently full," the robotic voice told her.

Stacey ended the call. Normally she would have been furious at her sister for not answering her phone and then having a full voicemail box. Yet she felt numb all over. All she could feel was the metallic taste of worry in her mouth.

It had all happened so quickly. Tina had seemed completely fine. How could they have been discussing storms one minute and then the next Tina was in the hospital? The image of Tina thrashing around, arms rigid and legs kicking, came back to Stacey. She closed her eyes.

She tried her sister again but to no avail. She was sure that Allison was busy trying to woo Jacob back into her spider's web. Sitting there, alone in the hospital waiting room, Stacey had never felt so alone.

When her parents died, Stacey and Allison were doing homework together. Even back then, Stacey tried to teach her sister by helping her with studies, but with little luck. The two sisters had been different from birth like the wind and the sea.

Stacey could recall that evening with perfect clarity. She could see Allison rolling her eyes at her. She could smell the cookies that Tina had just baked and was letting cool in the kitchen. They were with their grandmother because their parents had gone out to a party that night. Stacey could recall feeling pleased with herself because she had painted her nails for the first time by herself. It was a shiny pink color—glossy and applied as perfectly as Stacey could manage.

She had kept glancing at her nails as she lectured Allison. She liked the way they contrasted against the darkness of her skin. Allison had been so mad that she hadn't been allowed to paint her nails by herself yet. But their mother knew it would end up all over the kitchen table.

The TV was on in the living room. Tina and Burt, the girls' grandfather, were watching the local news. Burt had always smelled like cigars. It was a comforting scent to Stacey, even now. She remembered the phone suddenly ringing. The noise shattered the peaceful illusion of the night. In Stacey's mind, that phone ringing was when everything changed. It signalled the end of one chapter and the start of a terrible one.

Allison had gotten up to answer the phone. She had recently started using the phone to call friends as often as their parents permitted, much to their grandparents' chagrin. It seemed natural that her sister would think it was for her.

But it was Tina who had gotten to the phone first. She picked it up, waving Allison off. Then she asked for the caller to repeat the message.

Stacey could recall the sudden swoop of her stomach. Her pencil, hovering over her math homework, seemed frozen in the air. She had no reason

to suspect anything was wrong, yet there was
something off about how her grandmother was
speaking. Her tone was pitched up high, too high, and
then she placed the phone down to pick up the call in
her bedroom.

Burt had followed Tina, leaving the two sisters
alone. Allison began badgering her. Stacey had shushed
her, which just annoyed Allison.

Then she heard it, the crying from the bedroom. She
had never heard her grandmother make that sound
before. It was a keening wail that seemed to silence
Allison as if she had lost her voice. The two of them
stared at the bedroom.

When Burt came out to tell them that their parents
were killed, Stacey found that she couldn't look him in
the face. Instead, her gaze fell on the TV right behind
him. She stared at it, letting the images wash over her
as Allison sobbed.

The picture on the television was fuzzy and
sometimes would burst into static. Stacey watched it
silently.

Chapter Eight

Something snapped Stacey out of her memories. She felt as if she was dragging herself out of a pool filled with tar as she looked up. The waiting room was still empty. The TV shoved in the corner was playing the news. She was freezing cold sitting there in the small waiting room all alone.

The noises that jarred her were from two nurses walking by. They had clearly come from their break and were talking excitedly about something. The words seemed to slide in and out of her brain without registering.

Her fingers were curled around her phone. When Stacey opened her hand, her bones felt stiff. She wasn't sure how long she had been sitting there thinking about Tina and the night her parents died.

She tried calling Allison again, but the result was the same. She put her phone on the seat next to her and went back to staring at the floor. She had been trying for so long not to cry about the situation that she doubted the tears would come even if she wanted the relief the tears would bring.

Her phone vibrated. Without looking, Stacey answered.

"Finally," she said, although nagging Allison was more out of habit than anything else. "You need to get here to the hospital. It's Tina," her voice hitched. "Tina had a seizure or something."

"Stacey?"

A male voice jarred Stacey, and she looked down at her phone screen. She had answered an unknown number.

Tentatively she replied with, "Who is this?"

"Tony. I'm sorry to have called you. It was about work. Ms. Stark gave me your number but…" He paused and trailed off.

It took Stacey a few seconds for her mind to catch up with what Tony was saying. Out of everyone to call her, she hadn't been expecting it to be him.

"Oh, sorry. I didn't even look to see who was calling."

She had hoped that her voice sounded normal. She had tried to make it sound as if she hadn't answered the phone, word vomiting about her grandmother. But her voice ended up a pitch too high. It sounded false even to her own ears.

"Stacey, your grandmother… is she alright?" His tone was gentle and soft as if he was approaching a deer and trying not to scare it.

Maybe it was Tony's voice. Perhaps it was the fact that Stacey hadn't gotten through to Allison to talk about Tina being in the ICU that finally cracked the ice she had been trying to keep around her heart.

But instead of telling Tony everything was fine and she would call him back later, she let out a choked sob. Her tears came fast and furiously as she recalled the events to him.

Tony listened silently. She was sure that he thought she was crazy. What sort of person sobbed like this to their boss? But Stacey couldn't have stopped even if she wanted to.

When she finished, Tony asked, "You can't get in touch with your sister?"

"No. She's probably trying to fuck Jacob or something," she retorted tearfully.

Tony wasn't sure of the extent of Allison and Jacob's relationship and didn't ask. Instead, he said, "Stay there, okay?"

The call ended suddenly. Stacey stared down at the phone, which was now lifeless in her hand. Where else would she go? Out of habit she tried Allison again but got nothing. With little else to do, she did what Tony had asked. She stayed there. It wasn't as if she would leave Tina alone.

After some time, she was tracing a line in the carpet with her foot when she heard someone speak her name. Stacey looked up, hoping for a doctor or someone who would have an update on Tina.

But to her surprise, Tony stood there. She blinked a couple of times to make sure that she hadn't imagined it. But no, he was standing right next to her. He was wearing a regular t-shirt imprinted with a band name she didn't know. He had a pair of baggy jeans on. For once, his hair wasn't slicked back and was slightly messy. He was wet from the rain. In one hand, he was trying to cradle two coffees.

"Tony," Stacey breathed.

"That took longer than I thought. Rain slowed me down."

"What are you doing? Why are you here?" Stacey asked.

"You were alone. Your grandmother is in the hospital. I thought you could do with some company." Tony sat down next to her and handed her one of the cups.

"For me?"

"Of course. Unless you think I'm the sort of fool to carry two coffees around for myself."

Stacey gingerly took one from him. It was still hot. She held it in her hands, cradling it as she looked away from Tony. She hadn't been expecting this random act of kindness, especially from Tony of all people. The gesture touched her.

"It's mocha. I hope that's okay. I wasn't sure how you take it."

"No, this is perfect, thank you," Stacey replied.

Tony offered her a small smile as he took a sip of his own coffee. The two of them sat in silence for a few minutes. Stacey blew on her cup to cool it off as Tony sat next to her. His phone rang but he didn't check it or get up to take the call. Instead, he sent it to voicemail. They sat together in a strangely comfortable silence. Even though her heart was aching, having him with her made things a little better.

"I should try Allison again," Stacey finally mumbled.

"Still can't get hold of her?"

"No."

"Have you tried texting her?"

The question was a simple one but wasn't even something that Stacey had considered. Stacey's phone plan didn't cover texting. She considered it an expense that she didn't need. But that didn't mean her phone couldn't text.

"I'm an idiot. I should have…" she said as she brought up the text screen.

Tony's hand rested on her knee. She looked up at him. Her chest constricted for a moment. His eyes were kind.

"Don't be so hard on yourself."

She nodded, "Right. Yeah. It's just difficult."

She composed a text to Allison which felt as if it took twenty years to write. Since her phone was a simple flip phone, there was no fancy keyboard to type the message. After what felt like hours, she finally hit send.

"That might get her attention," Stacey admitted. "I don't think I have ever sent her a text before."

She waited a few seconds. She hoped that Allison would get her message and call. But her phone was as silent as ever. She took a sip of her coffee. The warmth of the beverage helped, especially since the hospital was so cold. Tony didn't look bothered by the fact he was wet and sitting in a chilly hospital waiting room.

Something struck Stacey, and she turned her head to look at him, "Why were you calling me?"

"I was going to see if you could work Saturday. Some of us are trying to finish up a last-minute media deal, and I needed someone to handle the front desk. But don't worry about that now."

"Oh, well thanks for thinking of me. I'm always trying to earn extra cash," Stacey said.

"I'll keep that in mind if I can get you more hours. I'll let Ms. Stark know before I leave."

"You're leaving?"

"Not for long. I have some business back home to attend to. I'll be gone for a week or two."

Tony's leaving made Stacey feel odd, although she couldn't pinpoint exactly why. Her head was starting to hurt and she didn't dwell on it. She rubbed her temples.

"You must be tired," he said to her.

"I am, but I'm not going anywhere until I know what is going on with my grandmother," Stacey replied.

"Let me try to find you a blanket, at least."

She nodded and yawned. As soon as Tony mentioned being tired, she could feel the exhaustion seeping into her bones.

By the time he returned with a blanket, Stacey was ready to fall asleep. Tony was draping the blanket over her, when a tall, pale thin man came out of the ICU and walked over to them. Stacey stood up, although she didn't know why. It just seemed as if she should be standing when he came into the waiting room.

He introduced himself as the doctor and then told Stacey of Tina's condition.

"We aren't sure what triggered the seizure yet. But she's going to pull through."

Relief swept through Stacey so hard and fast that she thought her legs were going to give out. Tony must have sensed her weakness because he had taken her elbow to steady her.

The doctor continued, "We want to keep her overnight for observation. We aren't sure how this is going to affect her brain."

"Yes, of course. Please. Can I see her?"

"Not yet. But I'll let you know when you can."

Stacey nodded, although she would have liked to see her grandmother immediately. She wanted to see her with her own eyes that Tina was going to pull through. As the doctor left, Stacey realized that Tony was still supporting her. She quickly pulled away.

"I'm glad she's going to be okay," Tony said to her.

"Me too. I'm just worried about her memory. It was already not that great. Now I am definitely going to have to get her proper medical care. What if this had happened when she was by herself?" She felt sick just thinking about it.

"Well, the good thing is that it didn't," Tony said to her. "So don't dwell on that."

Stacey didn't get a chance to reply. She heard someone rushing down the hallway. Her sister appeared as if conjured up by magic. Her hair was plastered to her head from the rain and she looked out of breath. Her eyes were wild and panicked as she looked around.

When she saw Stacey, she bolted over to her and crushed her in a hug. Not being able to recall the last time that she had hugged her sister, Stacey slowly returned it.

"She's going to be okay," Stacey whispered. "The doctor was just here."

"I am so fucking sorry that I didn't get your message," Allison said. "My phone was on silent. I just happened to check it when I went to the bathroom, and I saw you had texted me. I would have come here earlier if I had known."

"I know. It's okay."

The hug ended and Allison glanced at Tony. She frowned, probably wondering why in the world he was there.

Tony smiled. "I called her to ask something, and she thought it was you. I thought I would come by to keep her company in the meantime."

"How nice of you," Allison replied although there was a strange hitch in her voice that Stacey didn't understand.

"He brought coffee," Stacey added.

"Great. Can we see Tina yet?"

"Not yet. They'll let us know. They want to keep her overnight for observation."

Allison shook her head. "This is so fucked up. Can you believe this? Tell me exactly what happened."

Stacey launched into the story again. When she finished, Allison was fiddling with the hem of her skirt. Her sister was obviously with Jacob because she was dressed for a night out on the town.

"That's awful. I told you. I told you she needed to get placed into a nursing home or something," Allison accused.

"I know. But I couldn't afford it. And I was there."

"What if you weren't?" Allison demanded. "She has to be somewhere safe, Stacey. Not at home. We're going to have hospital bills out of the fucking ass to pay now, anyway."

Stacey hadn't thought of that. She had been so concerned with Tina that she hadn't thought of how little insurance would cover for this hospital stay. She could feel a headache threatening to pounce.

Allison kept going, "We have to find her a home to stay in. We can't risk that again. I won't let you."

She didn't have the energy to fight with Allison. She didn't have the energy to point out that money didn't grow on trees and she was doing what she could. Instead, she just gave into exhaustion. Her sister kept lecturing her as if she had done something wrong. She knew Allison was stressed out and upset by the way she was lashing out at Stacey.

But Tony didn't know that. He swiftly stepped in between the two of them.

"That's enough."

"Excuse me?" Allison snapped.

"This isn't Stacey's fault. It isn't anyone's fault. Your grandmother is going to pull through. The best thing you can do right now is work together."

Allison looked at Tony as if she couldn't believe the words coming out of his mouth. Then she looked over at Stacey.

"What is this? Is this the guy you're fucking?"

"Wow, really?" Stacey snapped, feeling an emotion that wasn't just numbness for the first time in hours.

Tony looked alarmed. "No, we aren't like that."

"Then why are you here? What sort of guy swoops on over with coffee like that? She just got out of seeing a guy. Step off."

"Allison!"

Tony looked abashed. "It isn't like that. I know she just got out of a thing with Charlie—"

Allison's gaze snapped back to Stacey. Oh shit, Stacey thought. She suddenly wished Tony had just kept his mouth shut.

"Charlie? You mean that asshole who tried to kick us out of the apartment complex? You were dating him?"

Tony went to speak again but her sister shoved past him. She was looking directly at Stacey now.

"Are you fucking kidding me, Stacey? You were seeing that guy, but kept getting on me for dating Jacob? Are you a hypocrite or just a jerk?"

"Neither," Stacey snapped, coming to life underneath her sister's judgmental gaze. "I had no idea who Charlie was."

"Oh, so that makes it alright? Did you leave as soon as you found out?"

When Stacey didn't reply, Allison threw her hands up in the air.

"Well, that answers that."

"We don't need to discuss this right now. It isn't important. We can talk about it later."

But her sister was shaking her head. "No way. You don't get to weasel your way out of this one."

Stacey was mortified that Allison was pressing this right now under the circumstances. She didn't feel like discussing Charlie in front of Tony. It felt wrong somehow as if she was flinging his kindness back in his face. So, she turned around and walked away, down the hospital hallway. If Allison was determined to fight about this, then Stacey wasn't going to let it happen in the waiting room in front of Tony.

Sure enough, Stacey could hear Allison following her down the hallway. She walked through the waiting room toward the ER and went outside. The rain was still coming down. It was coming down so hard that it slammed off the ground and the nearby cars, each droplet exploding.

They were under an overhang. Stacey stopped at the edge of it and turned around. It had cooled off considerably from the rain. It felt as if summer had been swept away in the storm. Allison crossed her arms. She was shooting daggers from her eyes.

"Just blurt out what you want to say and get over it," Stacey said simply.

"I just can't believe you. I really can't. This entire time you were hooking up with the guy who wanted us out on the streets. Not only that but how many times have you lectured me about my lifestyle? So, it's okay for you to chase rich men but not me?"

"I wasn't chasing him! I didn't even know who he was. I didn't seek it out. I wasn't trying to snag a rich guy to pay my way through life, Allison."

"How can you have stood there and nagged me about what I was doing with Jacob when you were doing the same thing? You always act so fucking holier-than-thou, Stacey. As if the way you live life is the right and proper way and the way I live is disgusting. But this entire time you weren't any better!"

"I am better!" Stacey snapped, finally bubbling over and having enough. "You really want to talk about this now while our grandmother is in the hospital? No, I had no idea who Charlie was. When I did, I wanted to break up with him. He saved our apartment complex just to have a shot with me, and I still broke up with him!"

Allison's eyes widened slightly but she didn't speak.

Stacey went on, "I broke up with him because that lifestyle he had with his family plotting and planning against him, and some woman thinking she was engaged to him—why would I want that? Money would solve all our problems—I know that! But it isn't enough for me to put up with the insanity that comes with that inner circle!"

"We are never going to have enough money, Stacey! Never! No matter how hard we work or how much we try, we aren't ever going to be secure, much less comfortable. I know you just got that new job so you're feeling as if everything is going to be easier now, but look," she gestured at the hospital, "Now Tina is going to need serious medical care and you're broke as hell again."

"So, what? What does that mean? That I'm just supposed to not try? Should I just run off and try to marry a rich guy? That doesn't solve anything either, Allison. Sure, you'll have money. But what else will you have? A guy who you pretended to like and changed yourself to be with. Why would I want that? Why would you want that? You're always selling yourself short. You think if you show someone who you really are, you'll be shot down."

"Now you know what I'm thinking and feeling? I'm so sick of butting heads with you! No matter what I do, it isn't good enough. Ever since Mom and Dad died, you think you know it all when it comes to me. But you aren't my mom. You don't have any control over me or what I do."

"Obviously," Stacey said through clenched teeth, "Since you have no fucking idea what you're doing."

Allison's jaw clenched, too. The two sisters stared at each other. Part of Stacey wished they were little kids again so it would be socially acceptable to tackle Allison to the ground and pull her hair.

"No, you don't get to do that anymore," Allison finally said. "You don't get to tell me how to live my life."

"Then get out."

"What?"

"Get out of the apartment. I don't want you there anymore. I always do this. I always do this shit for you. I let you crash at my place. I tolerate your poor life choices. I keep thinking one day you're going to wake up and realize there is more to life than fucking rich guys and trying to get their money. But you're right, it's your life. So, leave and live it."

Allison looked shocked. Stacey had surprised herself. She had never actually told Allison to leave before. It had always been some strange mutual understanding that her sister would constantly mess up her life and would crash on Stacey's couch.

But why? Why did she tolerate that? Stacey always bowed to whatever Allison wanted. Ever since they were kids, she had done it. But anytime they were together all they did was fight. It was no longer worth it.

Allison's shock quickly turned to anger. Her pretty features twisted, and she scowled. She didn't say anything. Instead, she just turned around and headed back inside the hospital.

Stacey watched her go, feeling empty and unmoored.

Chapter Nine

"This one is nice." Amanda slid the brochure over to Stacey.

Stacey picked it up and looked at it. It was a nursing home on the outskirts of the city. The photo showed a radiant nurse helping an old man out of his wheelchair. Something about the photo was so phony that all Stacey did was drop it back onto the table.

"Let me see it. I'll look it up." Tony took the brochure off the table.

It had been four days since Tina had her seizure. She was still in the hospital for observation. Stacey had spoken to her grandmother for the first time after the first night of observation. It hadn't been uplifting. Tina had been distant and foggy. She had a difficult time remembering recent events. She kept asking Stacey if she was still considering going to college—something she hadn't considered for many years now. When Tina asked for Allison, Stacey tried to keep the bitter tone out of her voice that her sister wasn't there.

In fact, when Stacey finally made it home that first night, Allison's things were gone. Her sister left the hospital an hour before Stacey did. She must have gone by the apartment and cleared everything out. The living room couch was stripped of all blankets and pillows. Her clothes were yanked out of Tina's dressers. The bathroom was clear of the makeup piles and perfume sets Allison cherished.

It was as if Allison had never been there. Stacey wanted to feel the loss, but she was so stressed and concerned about Tina that Allison's leaving without saying goodbye was the last thing on her mind. She was too drained to think about it.

Now she was sitting at the small dining room table with brochures of nursing homes splayed in front of her. Amanda had come by to help. To her surprise, so had Tony. He had been a constant presence since the first night at the hospital. He would leave for a few hours a day to tend to business and then would return to her place again to check on her.

Normally, Stacey would have protested. She would have told Tony it wasn't necessary to keep coming back to spend time with her. But he was giving her time off from work and offering a shoulder to lean on. With Allison gone, she needed the support more than she could admit to herself. So, she took it without question or protest.

"This place doesn't have a great rating online," Tony said from behind his laptop.

He was looking up reviews of places where Tina could live. Stacey appreciated it. She didn't own a laptop and felt too frenzied to do her own research at the library. Having Tony look it up and tell her up front if the place was solid or not had helped out a lot.

"Forget it," she said.

Amanda took the brochure and threw it in the trash. "Moving on."

"Guys, this is starting to look hopeless," Stacey mumbled, running her hand over her face.

"Only because you're emotional and want the best for your grandmother like anyone would," Amanda pointed out.

Tony nodded. "She's right. You want Tina to go somewhere nice so you're bound to overthink it. You want the best for her, it's only natural."

"I want the best, but can't afford it," she sighed.

Amanda's phone rang. She excused herself and left the dining room. Stacey looked down at the brochures. All of them were blending together. Very gently, Tony's hand covered hers. The touch of his skin sent a flash of warmth through her. Stacey looked up at him, startled.

His smile was kind, "It'll come together. Don't worry."

"It's hard not to worry. I told myself I wouldn't ever send my grandmother off somewhere. I would take care of her myself. And now look—I'm trying to find a place to dump her."

"You're not dumping her. You're doing the right thing, Stacey. I know you want the best for her. And this is the best."

Stacey nodded and mulled his words over in her head. Her gaze settled on the way his hand covered hers. There was something comforting about his touch. Her heart was beating quickly for the first time in a while for a reason other than fear.

She heard Amanda end the phone call and pulled her hand away. She got up from the table.

"I need something to drink. What about you?" she said quickly, hoping the fact she was blushing wasn't evident.

Before Tony could answer, she went to the kitchen to find drinks. She scolded herself for letting herself feel that pull toward Tony. She had bigger things to worry about. Acting like a schoolgirl wouldn't help anything.

"What do you think?" Tony asked her.

Stacey looked around the garden. The sun was poking through the clouds which were threatening yet again with another summer storm. Even though everything looked dreary and dark, the garden was still pretty. There were fresh flowers in a well-maintained garden, as well as trees that were tall and healthy looking. Benches were stationed around the garden for people to read or just enjoy the day. A couple of chess tables were under one of the largest trees. Two men were hunched over, trying to finish the game before the clouds let loose.

"I love it."

It was true. She did love it. Not just the garden, but the entire nursing home. It seemed to be exactly what Stacey wanted for her grandmother. She had been impressed by the rooms and the nurses. She liked the activities they had for the residents. Even the décor was bright and cheery.

"I mean, from start to finish, everything in it is amazing," she went on, "in fact, I want to move here myself."

Tony laughed at her joke. If she had thought three weeks ago that Tony would have been the one to drive her forty minutes away to check this nursing home out, Stacey would have thought she was crazy.

But the drive had been enjoyable. With Tina still in the hospital and her memory seemingly worse than ever, Stacey was on the brink of a serious crying jag when Tony suggested the trip. She had agreed just to get out of the city and look around.

"Of course, she can't stay here."

"Why not?" Tony asked.

"I looked at the prices. I can't afford to put Tina here. If I had known how expensive this place was, I wouldn't have bothered making the trip."

Tony had been checking one of the activity rooms when Stacey had inquired about the cost. It was completely out of her price range. This place was state of the art and one of the best nursing homes in the state.

"I feel bad that I made you waste your time like this."

Tony shook his head, "It wasn't a waste of time."

There was something in his tone of voice that gave her pause. It had been like that a lot recently. There were light touches from him, like his hand on the small of her back guiding her into rooms, or a casual brush against her hands. Every time he did that, Stacey felt herself instantly react. Her heart seemed to thrum and her throat would tighten.

Yet she hadn't entertained the idea of doing anything with Tony. Perhaps if life hadn't been so messy already, she would have thought that he was interested in her. But the odds of two billionaires being interested in her was too comical for her to consider.

"How wasn't it?" she asked as the sky lit up suddenly with the first lightning strike.

Tony reached out for her. His arm entwined with hers as he pulled her toward the nursing home to get her out of the incoming storm.

"You have a better idea of what you're looking for in regard to Tina," he said as they entered one of the activity rooms.

The woman who had been showing them around appeared by Stacey's side. "Glad you guys got in before the storm! So, what do you think?"

"It's perfect but I'm going to have to think about it," Stacey lied swiftly before Tony could mention money.

"Of course. We understand it is a big decision to make." The woman beamed at her as they followed her toward the lobby.

They said goodbye once they reached the front entrance, and Tony held the door open for her. The sky had darkened considerably in the few minutes they had spent inside. It looked as if it was going to crack open at any moment and pour rain down on them.

"The storms this summer are crazy," Stacey remarked.

"I should have brought an umbrella or parked closer. Want me to pull the car up?"

"No, it's okay," she said, feeling too uncomfortable to ask Tony to do that for her. "We can just walk quickly."

They set off across the parking lot. Earlier, when they had arrived at the facility, it was during the peak visiting time. Because of the increased visitors, the parking lot had been filled. Tony had parked way in the back.

As they hurried across toward the car, the clouds decided they had had enough and opened up. One second Stacey was dry as a bone, the next it was almost as if she had dropped herself into a swimming pool.

The rain soaked through her clothes, and she gasped in surprise. It was freezing cold.

Next to her, Tony let out a laugh. She couldn't imagine laughing. She was sure his clothes today—which consisted of a simple white dress shirt and a pair of khakis—were probably designer-made. She would have been in tears after getting expensive clothes ruined by rain.

But his laughter softened his features as he pulled her toward the car. Her clothes were completely drenched in a matter of seconds. When they finally arrived at his car, Stacey couldn't help it. She began to laugh as well.

It was the first time she had laughed this hard in ages. The sight of Tony, laughing, soaked to the bone and apparently not bothered by the torrential downpour struck her as humorous for some inane reason. She just stood there, resting against his car, letting the rain belt against her as she laughed.

It was a welcomed reprieve to feel something that hadn't been frustration, pain, or anger. It was as if she had been swimming in those emotions lately. Laughing with Tony over seemingly nothing was freeing.

She looked up at him and their laughs suddenly died. Before Stacey could do anything, Tony was moving toward her. His fingers were tilting her chin up to meet his eyes. Her breath caught.

Then he brought his lips down onto hers. The kiss was soft and probing as if he was expecting her to pull away.

But Stacey didn't pull away. She returned the kiss. The rain pelted against her skin. Goosebumps broke out across her body. She could feel Tony's wet clothes against her. His lips were warm even in this weather.

The kiss deepened. His hands went around her waist. She pulled him against her as she leaned against his car. His hair was messy as she trailed her fingers through it.

Tony moved an inch away from her and breathed, "I've been wanting to do that for quite a while."

She blinked water out of her eyes and tried to hide her smile. She had wanted it as well. She just had never expected him to make the move.

"We should head back now," she finally said, "before we both catch colds."

Tony laced his fingers through hers and said, "Sounds good to me."

Chapter Ten

Stacey looked out the window of Tina's hospital room. For once, it wasn't raining. The sky was hazy, the sun blocked by clouds. It was overcast and muggy outside, a strange mix of summer and storms.

Tina was watching a daytime soap opera from her hospital bed. Her figure looked somehow skinnier and more fragile than when Stacey had seen her yesterday. Her eyes were glassy and her voice muted. They had barely spoken since Stacey's arrival twenty minutes ago.

"It's really warm outside today," Stacey said in an attempt to jumpstart the conversation again.

Tina nodded but didn't reply. Stacey could feel her chest constrict. Whatever the seizure had done to Tina had been intense with little chance she would bounce back from it.

Stacey spoke again, "Allison is gone. Has she come by to see you? I asked her to leave the apartment."

It was something she normally wouldn't have told her grandmother. She had tried to shield her from the fights she had with her sister once Tina's memory started to worsen. But Stacey thought instead of sugar coating the conversations, she would try to be brutally honest.

And it seemed to work. Tina turned her head slightly to look over at Stacey, whose heart lifted.

"Allison never finished her homework. You tell your sister… you tell her what she needs to do."

Then she turned back to the TV. Stacey watched Tina with the hope lessening in her chest. She knew that Tina needed constant medical care in a nursing home. But she couldn't find one that was solid that would also fall into her price range.

The place that she had seen with Tony had been a dream come true. She told herself not to dwell on it any longer. She couldn't put Tina there. Not with hospital bill debt about to be racked up.

She had told Tony that much on the drive home the other day. After they had kissed, it was as if a dam had burst between them. During the car ride, they had swapped stories about growing up. He talked about his grandfather who had suffered a stroke and ultimately passed away when Tony was a teen. It felt as if he understood why she wanted to take care of Tina and not just lock her away somewhere awful and forget about her.

Even with everything going on, she found herself thinking back to the kiss with Tony. It had been a picture-perfect kiss. The sort of kiss Stacey had seen in movies and had never dreamt she would experience herself.

She wanted to kiss him again. She could hear Allison's voice in her head, calling her all sorts of names over the fact she had kissed Tony. But she pushed it out of her mind. Her sister was gone—running back to Jacob or whatever new billionaire she was trying to snag.

"Stacey."

Her grandmother's voice snapped her back to the present. She stood up and went over to Tina's bedside. Stacey grabbed Tina's hand and held it gently. Her skin felt like wrinkled paper, and she looked old. It was as if she had aged twenty years in less than a week.

"Yes?"

"Don't blame yourself. It isn't your fault that I'm here."

A moment of clarity. That was what her grandmother was experiencing. The doctor had told her this would happen sometimes.

"I need to get you better care," Stacey said quickly as if the clock was running against her. "I need to get people to watch over you all the time."

Tina patted her hand, "I know. You always know what to do. Your moral compass… it always pointed North. Strong and true. Just like your mama."

Tears sprung into Stacey's eyes. She could feel a lump in her throat. Stacey blinked past tears but it was impossible. She could feel them fall down her cheeks.

Tina smiled a little and said, "Your sister was here earlier."

"She was?"

"Yes. She said you two fought. You two were always fighting ever since I can remember. You two are so different. But after I'm gone—"

"Don't talk like that," Stacey said, panicked.

"After I am gone," she repeated firmly, "you two need to take care of each other. You must watch out for one another no matter what. You're sisters. No matter what."

"I know. I know you're right. She's just…"

"Different from you," Tina whispered, "I know this. But Allison will find her way someday. You just need to be patient."

Stacey nodded, unable to speak. It was as if all the air had been sucked out of her lungs. To hear Tina talk about after she was gone, put things in dreadful perspective. Her fear of losing her grandmother seemed to wreak havoc within her stomach. For a second, Stacey was worried she was going to be sick.

Then Tina let out a yawn. Her eyelids looked droopy as if she was going to fall asleep on the spot.

"Are you tired from the meds?" Stacey asked.

"That's right," she mumbled.

Stacey didn't get a chance to reply. Tina's eyes closed as she drifted off to sleep. Stacey stood there and watched Tina sleep. Her chest ached. She didn't have anyone else in this world. It was impossible to deny. But she had always considered Tina to be the one solid force in her life.

Losing her parents had been such a brutal stab to her heart. Even now, when she thought about her mom and dad, sometimes the sadness threatened to engulf her. It was her grandparents who had stopped her from completely losing it as a child.

But her grandfather was gone now. All that remained was Tina. To lose her was going to be a terrible thing no matter if it was ten minutes or ten years from now.

After watching her sleep for a few moments, Stacey left the room. The thought of going back to her apartment depressed her. She wasn't used to being completely alone there.

The muggy summer air hit her as she left the hospital. It was still cloudy and looked as if it would rain again at any moment. Yet the air was hot and made her clothes stick to her skin. She checked her phone to see if Tony had called her.

There were no calls from Tony, but there was a missed call from a number she didn't know. When she listened to the voicemail, she heard a message from a woman who worked at the nursing home Stacey had gone to see with Tony.

Confused, she returned the call and leaned against the hospital wall. A proper sounding woman picked up on the third ring and introduced herself as the admissions agent.

"I'm just a little confused," Stacey said after introducing herself, "I didn't fill out any information about sending my grandmother there."

"Are you sure? We received everything this morning including payment in advance for five years."

"What?"

"Everything is set up and paid for through AAC Investments. Is that not correct?"

Stacey clutched her phone tightly as her head swam. For a brief crazy second, she had thought perhaps Tony had set it up. It had made sense, hadn't it? He had been there with her. But the name of the company that had set it up and paid in advance sounded like one of Charlie's companies.

"Can I call you back?" she said quickly and hung up before the woman could reply.

Charlie had known about Tina. She knew that information was swift and rapid in their little, closed circle. If Tony had mentioned it to anyone about her grandmother, Charlie could have heard.

Even so, Stacey ended up dialing Tony's number.

"Stacey! I was just about to call you."

"Hey, sorry to bother you. I have a weird question. Did you tell anyone about my grandmother being in the hospital?"

"Well, yes, I had to let certain people at the office know why you were leaving for a while. Ms. Stark knew."

"What about anyone else?"

"Oh, did Charlie call you? I told him about the nursing home and Tina but only because he was there—"

"I have to go. I'll call you back."

"Wait, Stacey! Did you—"

But Stacey had already hung up. It was Charlie then who had overstepped and given her this gift to woo her back. But there was no way she could take this. She didn't want to have anything to do with him and she thought she made that clear the last time she spoke to him. There was no way she could accept his paying for five years at the nursing home.

She debated calling him and telling him that she couldn't accept it. But Tony had mentioned that Charlie was still in town. Stacey would go to him directly and tell him she couldn't let him pay for her financial conundrum.

<<◇>>

When Stacey arrived at Charlie's apartment, she realized belatedly that she wasn't getting past security.

She had forgotten how state-of-the-art everything was. So much for cornering him unaware.

Feeling out of place among such luxury, Stacey went to the front desk. She gave her name to the receptionist and asked to see Charlie. The woman looked her up and down as if wondering why someone like Stacey was there. Stacey felt exposed and vulnerable in front of this well-dressed pint-sized woman but kept her gaze level.

After a couple of minutes on the phone, the woman looked up, looking surprised.

"He says you can go up now."

Stacey thanked her and headed toward the elevators. She pressed the penthouse button and felt the elevator lift her up toward Charlie. Now that she was about to see him, she felt incredibly nervous.

She hadn't seen him since she had broken up with him. He hadn't tried to call her or reach out in any way. Stacey should have known that he was planning some major gesture to try to convince her to give him another chance.

The doors to the elevator glided open. Charlie was already waiting for her. The sight of him knocked the breath out of her. She had seemingly forgotten how perfect he was. He had some stubble across his face, but other than that, he was unchanged. His hair was messy. The sleeves of his dress shirt were unfolded and hung around his wrists.

"Stacey," he said, "I have to admit that this is quite a surprise."

Stacey willed herself to step off the elevator. She forced herself to look into his eyes.

"I need to talk to you. About what you did."

He looked confused for a moment. "What I did?"

"With my grandmother."

Charlie still looked lost. She wondered why he was acting as if he didn't know what she was talking about. She sighed.

"Charlie, stop. I know you paid for Tina's nursing home care. But I can't accept your gift. Please call them and change it. Get your money back. I'll figure something out but I can't take your money."

Charlie didn't seem to have the reaction that Stacey expected. All he did was stare at her as if she had three heads. Stacey was going to say more but cut herself off and crossed her arms defensively.

"Stacey, while I am touched that you think I have stepped into this situation to help you out, I'm afraid you're mistaken."

"What?"

He shrugged, "I didn't set up Tina at any nursing home nor put any money toward it. I don't know who did, but it wasn't me. Sorry you came all this way for that."

Stacey could only stare. The rest of her speech died before it could leave her lips. She had been planning on telling him how she couldn't take his money especially since they weren't together, and how they both needed to move on but all she could do was feel extremely embarrassed.

Charlie moved toward her. He was very close to her now. Up that close, she could recall how his lips felt on hers. The thought made her look away from him.

"I have to admit that it is nice seeing you again," he said very softly.

His voice made the hair on the back of her neck stand up. She could feel his breath brush against her cheek gently. It made her head swim to be this close to him again. Stacey was about to topple off that cliff and leaned forward to kiss him in a moment of weakness when a thought hit her out of the blue.

"Tony."

Confusion crossed Charlie's features, "What?"

"Tony. It was Tony who must have paid for it. That's what he was trying to tell me on the phone," Stacey thought aloud. "I have to go. I'm sorry to have bothered you."

Before Charlie could say anything else, she had spun around and was back in the elevator. The last thing she saw as the doors closed was Charlie standing there with an emotion on his face that she couldn't quite pinpoint.

Stacey tried to reach Tony as she headed back home, but he didn't pick up. She felt as if she had some sort of emotional whiplash. From finding out someone had paid for Tina to be at the nursing home, to being that close to Charlie, and finally to realizing that it was Tony who paid.

It had come to her right before she could kiss Charlie. Of course, it had made the most sense. Tony had been there. Even though Charlie was capable of such a huge gesture, Stacey hadn't heard from him since the break-up.

Why had she jumped to thinking it was Charlie instead of Tony? Tony had even tried to talk to her on the phone. He was probably trying to tell her it was him when she had hung up. Yet she had convinced herself that it had been Charlie.

Because she wanted to see him again, a little nagging voice in the back of her head said. As much as Stacey wanted to ignore it, she knew it was the truth. She had completely convinced herself Charlie was the one who had come to the rescue.

She would have kissed him. If her brain hadn't gotten its shit together, she would have leaned forward and kissed him. Would he have been upset if she had? Stacey doubted it. She had a sneaking feeling he would have kissed her anyway.

Stacey stepped off the bus and got inside the dingy apartment lobby just as the skies opened yet again.

Leon was in the lobby, checking the mail for his mother. He looked over at her when she entered.

"How is Tina?" he asked—everyone in the complex had seen Tina loaded into the ambulance.

"She's been better."

"There's some guy waiting for you outside your apartment."

"What?" Stacey exclaimed.

Leon shrugged and pulled out a pack of cigarettes from his pocket. She was too distracted to ask when he had started smoking or to lecture him about it.

"He's Asian."

Tony. Stacey said thanks and hurried upstairs. She was glad he was there because she wanted to speak to him about Tina. Although she wished that he would have given her some warning instead of just dropping by.

Tony was leaning against the wall by her front door. He was dressed casually and was looking at something on his phone.

"Hey."

He looked up and smiled. "You ran off on the phone earlier. You didn't speak to Charlie, did you? He must have been awfully confused if you mentioned the nursing home."

"It was you, wasn't it?" Stacey asked, avoiding his question.

"Of course, it was me!" Tony said and took her by the hands, pulling her close. "I saw how much you loved that place. It would be perfect for your grandmother. I took care of the hospital bills too."

Stacey made a noise that was a mix of surprise and dismay. Tony watched her with his eyes lighting up at her reaction. His smile grew.

"Come on. Let's get inside," he said, casting a glance around the tiny hallway.

Stacey nodded, unable to speak. She unlocked the door and Tony followed her. Like every other recent time she entered her apartment, the silence covered her like a blanket. At night, she tossed and turned, thinking about what it would be like to live in that silence forever.

Tony sat down on the couch and patted the seat. Stacey sat next to him and tried to prepare a speech in her head to tell him there was no way she could accept his gift.

But Tony spoke first, "I know you're going to want to refuse my offer. But it isn't a big deal for me. Paying the bills and putting your grandmother in that home is enough reward for me, truly. I don't mind a bit."

Stacey chewed her bottom lip. "That's a lot of money."

"I guess," he shrugged.

She studied his face as the realization came over her. It was a lot of money to her. To Tony, it was probably nothing more than a drop in the bucket. He had billions of dollars. Of course, he didn't think twice about it.

"I don't know what to say."

"You don't have to say anything," Tony replied. "This is what friends do for each other."

Friends. After the kiss, she hadn't been expecting to hear that word. She wasn't sure what they were anymore. Tony's hand moved toward her face and his fingertips ran underneath her chin. The touch made her heart skip a beat. She looked up at him.

"Friends, unless you would like to be more," he whispered.

For the second time that day, Stacey imagined toppling off a cliff. In saying yes to Tony, Charlie would be shelved for good. There would be no dreaming about him, day or night because Stacey would be committed to Tony and only him.

And when she searched his deep dark eyes, Charlie flew from her mind completely. Her lips pressed against Tony's as she answered his question with her touch. Yes, she would have him to herself. He had been there with her through all these dark times. He had come in like a knight in shining armor to support her. Hadn't she felt that connection with him right at the start?

Tony's kisses grew more urgent. His fingers trailed down her back as he pressed himself against her. Stacey could feel herself reacting to his touch. His lips brushed across her neck toward her lips until they locked, his tongue probing her mouth.

"The bedroom?" he whispered in between breaths.

She grabbed his hand and led him to her room. Through her lust, she remembered that her room was a mess. She had even thrown a blanket over her wall-length mirror in a fit of low self-esteem the other night. Tony cast a glance around the room. She couldn't read his expression.

But he didn't say anything. Instead, he pulled her close. Her hair had been thrown up into a ponytail but he yanked it out, his fingers tangling in her hair as he kissed her again.

Their clothes came off quickly, dropping in a heap on the floor. Stacey felt herself blushing in front of him as he pulled her down on the bed with him. He rolled on top of her and fondled her breasts.

Stacey closed her eyes, trying to lose herself in the sensation of him. But her mind kept spinning. It was flitting around to how odd it was to be there in her room with Tony. She had barely noticed her room when she had brought Charlie in there.

At the sudden thought of Charlie, she pushed him completely out of her mind. Tony made her feel things too. She was just nervous.

As if to expel all the negative thoughts haunting her mind, Stacey grabbed Tony and kissed him hard. Their lips crushed together and he let out a soft moan of surprise. She could feel his hard cock against her thigh.

There was no foreplay. Tony parted her thighs and entered her swiftly. Stacey closed her eyes and gasped in pleasure. He rocked inside of her, slowly at first, then more urgently. His tongue flicked across her nipples as he eagerly moved inside her.

"I love your body," he mumbled at one point.

Stacey wrapped her arms around him and tried to match his thrusts. Tony moved harder, bucking his hips hard against hers. He was moaning now and slightly out of breath, giving her small little noises of pleasure as he fucked her.

Tony thrust harder and then let out a shuddering gasp. He was climaxing, Stacey realized. His eyes were closed tightly as he came. Then he rolled off her and lay there.

Stacey blinked. She wasn't sure how she was feeling. She had just been getting worked up when he had finished. She knew it was unfair to compare lovers to other lovers, but yet.

He turned his head to hers and smiled. "That was amazing."

"Yeah, it was great," she lied.

Tony sat up. Stacey watched him, admiring his body. He was fantastically good looking. Today had been a long day. Maybe she should just give him the benefit of the doubt regarding his performance. It seemed unfair to rule him out just because this one time had been less than satisfying.

"I have a meeting to go to, but listen," he said as he picked up his clothes, "There's a birthday party for a friend of mine this weekend. Will you come with me?"

"Yeah, sure."

"Great. I'll call you with the details."

He leaned over and kissed her. Stacey returned the kiss. He smiled at her and said goodbye. She watched him leave and then stared at the ceiling until she heard the front door close.

Stacey tried to pinpoint her feelings. Surely, she was happy that she was seeing Tony now. She had felt that connection with him from that first night on the yacht. He had single-handedly helped her out with Tina and the mounting bills. She always enjoyed herself around him.

And now she was going with him to an event. An event filled with other people way outside her social status. She could feel the anxiety bubbling up inside of her. She would be out of her comfort zone again. She could practically see the elite of the elite staring at her as if she was some poor little thing that Tony had taken pity on.

She sat up and decided to shower. She wasn't going to dwell on this. She would go to the party with Tony and have a nice time. She deserved a nice time with everything else going on.

Chapter Eleven

"Wow, the room has a view of the garden too, Tina," Stacey said, looking out of the window.

Tina was in a wheelchair, having been too tired to walk. The taxi ride from the hospital to the apartment to pack up her things and then to the nursing home had been long. It had also been extremely emotional for Stacey.

But her grandmother hadn't seemed to sense the change that was going on around her. The doctors had warned Stacey that Tina was in the early stages of dementia and that a home was the best environment for her. Even so, Stacey was surprised to see just how much worse Tina had gotten since the seizure. It was as if the seizure, severe as it was, had wiped out the last remaining solid hold her grandmother had on her memory.

"Yes, the garden view was requested," their nurse, Rebecca, said.

Tony. Yet again he had been thinking things through for her. She had told him before how much Tina loved sitting in the garden at the apartment complex. Now she was close to one here as well. It was just more proof of how thoughtful he was.

"It's beautiful," Stacey repeated.

Tina was sitting upright in the wheelchair, looking around curiously. Her eyes were a little foggy. The worst part, Stacey was learning, was the moments of clarity.

There had been a moment of clarity when they were packing up Tina's clothes. Tina was sitting on the bed and was holding onto a sweater. When she looked up at Stacey, she looked almost sad.

"Is Allison coming by?"

"No, don't think so," Stacey had replied, folding a shirt.

She still hadn't heard from her sister. She wasn't sure where she was. She had called and let Allison know the name and address of the facility where Tina was moving but hadn't heard anything back. She wasn't going to refuse to tell Allison what was going on with their grandmother. She just thought that her sister would have gotten back to her.

"She'll come around," Tina said. She had been saying it a lot the last couple of days almost as if it was a chant.

Stacey hadn't replied. She wasn't feeling as confident as her grandmother about her sister's behavior. She couldn't see Allison returning, having some sense knocked into her head.

"Stacey," Tina said, "you'll come visit?"

It was the first time that she had shown awareness to what was going on and where she was going. Stacey put down the shirt she was folding and sat next to Tina.

"Of course. Whenever I can."

"So many changes," Tina said sadly. "All so quickly."

"I know. But we'll get through them together."

Tina brushed a lock of hair away from Stacey's face and spoke again, "Your parents would be proud of you, Stacey."

Stacey could feel the tears threatening again. She didn't want to cry, not now and with everything going on. She forced herself to smile and then kissed Tina on the cheek.

Tina looked around the room and then back at Stacey, "What were we talking about?"

It was one of those moments where Stacey felt the bottom drop out beneath her. The moments where Tina was there one second and then the next second, she was gone, had Stacey crashing back to earth. Her grandmother was sick. It was something she wished she could forget but knew she never could.

"Well, take your time getting settled," Rebecca said, snapping Stacey out of her thoughts. "I can go over some things with you when you're ready.

"Yeah, of course. Thanks."

Rebecca nodded and left them alone. The door was still open. In the hallway, Stacey could see a man in a walker heading slowly toward Tina's room. Even though the place was nice, it smelled slightly of antiseptic with a hint of mothballs. Seeing Tina in her wheelchair in the strange environment was upsetting her more than she had expected.

Stacey sat on the edge of Tina's bed. Her grandmother was fiddling with her wedding ring and looking around the room.

"What do you think?"

"It's very nice but when are we going home, dear? I'm very sleepy."

Stacey took her grandmother's hand and said quietly, "Tina, this is home now. Remember? We discussed it. We've been discussing it for a few days. This is where you are going to live from now on. But don't worry!" She tried to make her voice sound chipper, "I'm going to be here for you. I'll be visiting you every spare moment I can."

Tina's lips parted, but she didn't speak. She looked as if she was trying to recall when they had discussed her moving into a nursing home. After a couple of seconds, she closed her lips and nodded.

"Alright."

Stacey wasn't sure if Tina actually remembered the conversation or not. It was hard to tell if she truly remembered or was lying that she did.

"Now, let's finish unpacking your things." Stacey stood up and forced herself to smile.

In the parking lot, Stacey sat behind the wheel of her car. Tony was able to negotiate a good deal on the vehicle for her. With her new job and Tina's nursing care taken care of, Stacey was able to afford the additional monthly payments. The new ride would help save her a lot of time with her busy schedule and the distance Stacey needed to travel in order to visit Tina regularly.

The parking lot was almost empty. She was freezing as if her entire body was covered in ice. She stared at the place where Tina now lived.

For the millionth time in the last five minutes, she had to remind herself why this was good for her grandmother. Tina would have people watching her all the time now. There would be activities and more social interaction than Stacey could have provided.

Even so, some part of her—some small, unfair part of her—thought she was being selfish. Hadn't she told herself she would take care of her grandmother no matter what? Now Tina was in a home and Stacey was driving away like a mother who had sent her child off to summer camp.

Stop it, she told herself, *don't do this to yourself*. It accomplished nothing to do this to herself, yet it felt like a scab that Stacey kept picking.

Finally, she left the facility parking lot and headed back into town. There were no calls from Allison. Stacey couldn't believe that she hadn't come by to see Tina. Anger bubbled in her chest. Yes, she had kicked Allison out of the apartment. But that didn't mean Allison had to desert Tina.

As Stacey drove, she tried to push out all thoughts of Allison and Tina so that she wouldn't drive herself absolutely crazy. She was seeing Tony tonight. It was his friend's birthday party.

Stacey was itching to cancel going to the event. She didn't feel like seeing anyone. She wanted to curl up in bed and maybe watch television all night. But she had promised Tony, and the guilt from cancelling would be too much of a burden.

Yesterday he had sent her a dress to wear to the party. It was a beautiful dress of black and red. The fabric was so lovely that Stacey had been almost afraid to touch it. The card had said the dress was for the party and that he was excited to take her to it. She would hate to tell him this late that she had no interest in going. Not after everything he had done for her, for Tina.

By the time Stacey got home, she was ready for a shower. The hot water pounding against her skin lessened her nervousness a bit. After the shower, she stood staring at herself in the mirror.

What did Tony like about her body? When they had sex, he had said he liked it. But Stacey still didn't understand why. The longer she stood and stared at her shape, running her fingers over her breasts and the extra weight on her that she sometimes loathed, she could feel the nervousness return.

The dress fit her very well. Tony had somehow known her size. She had been worried the dress would cling to her in all the wrong places but the red stood out beautifully against her dark skin.

Her phone hummed. It was a text message from Tony.

"Going to be a little late so I've sent a car to pick you up. See you there."

Stacey could feel anxiety roll through her. She had been hoping to relax with Tony on the drive over. Now she was going to ride in the car there by herself and enter the party alone. She felt abandoned and uncomfortable just thinking about it.

Chapter Twelve

Stacey left the apartment and went downstairs to wait outside. For once in many days, the nighttime sky was clear of storms. The car that Tony sent rolled up to the curb right on time. The driver opened the door and Stacey slid into the back seat.

Soft classical music was playing. She closed her eyes and tried to focus on the music as the car took her to the party venue, outside the city limits. There was an entire section with homes so massive, her entire apartment could probably fit into a closet.

As the car stopped in front of a gated community, Stacey peered out the window. The windows in the car were tinted, so luckily she could gawk and no one would see her. Mansions lined the street. Some of them were two or three stories tall. *Imagine having all that space to yourself!* Just the thought of all those bedrooms made Stacey wonder what she would do with so much space.

There was a house at the end of the street that had a circular driveway. It was two stories tall with a balcony overlooking the neighborhood. Limousines and town cars were pulling up in front. Stacey held her breath, checked her hair, and smoothed her dress.

The car pulled up in the circular driveway and the driver got out to open her door. Before she knew it, she was stepping out in front of the house. She looked around the driveway. People in gorgeous clothes were heading to the front door. She didn't see Tony anywhere.

Holding the invitation in her hand that had come with the dress, Stacey went to the front door and handed it to the man who was greeting guests. He nodded and motioned her to enter.

She was in the foyer. If Stacey had been amazed by Charlie's penthouse, then this foyer was that times ten. It had marble floors with a winding staircase to the second floor. A stunning statue of a woman holding a vase graced the entranceway. Stacey stopped in her tracks to admire it. She hoped no one noticed that her jaw had dropped.

A small crowd had formed in the foyer. People were greeting each other like long-lost friends. Others were taking photos to capture the moment. Stacey felt left out and wriggled through the crowd to get through the foyer.

The foyer opened into a large room with different arches leading to other rooms. Ahead of her seemed to be a massive kitchen. To the right was the living room or den with a TV so large that Stacey couldn't believe such a thing was real. To the left was a sitting room of sorts, brimming with people.

Stacey started to panic. No matter where she went, she was going to look like a misfit, having no friends among the guests. It was like the few times Allison dragged her to similar parties. Stacey had always felt unsure of herself in the corner as her sister soaked up the attention.

"There you are."

She turned around to see Tony. Relief hit her hard. The tension in her shoulders lessened at the sight of him. He was dressed in a suit and looked incredibly handsome. He was smiling at her as he grabbed her hand.

"I am so sorry that I couldn't pick you up personally. I thought I was going to be much later than this. But I'm here now and only about five minutes late."

"Yeah, I'm glad you're here. I don't know anyone," Stacey whispered.

"No problem. I'll introduce you around."

And he did. Stacey spent the next hour swept up in talking to people she would have normally never spoken to. It made her a little dizzy to see all those people discussing things she knew very little about.

She was about to tell Tony as much and ask if she could grab a drink and go outside for air when he frowned at something over her head.

"Isn't that your sister?"

Stacey turned around to look at what he was talking about. To her amazement, Allison had just walked into the sitting room. She was dressed in a dark purple dress that brought out her pretty eyes and gripped her hips just right. Her hair was twisted up in a bun that accentuated her heart-shaped face.

On her arm was Jacob. He was as pale as ever with his hair combed back in such a way that it highlighted his receding hairline instead of masking it. Allison looked radiant next to him as if she had scored the most gorgeous guy ever as her escort.

Before Stacey could stop herself, she marched across the room. Allison's eyes fell on her and widened in surprise. Stacey gripped her sister's arm.

"I need to talk to you, please," she said through clenched teeth.

Allison allowed herself to be pulled away from Jacob. Stacey weaved through the crowd until they entered a smaller room near the kitchen. It was filled with paintings and opened to the patio. Luckily no one else was there. It allowed them a little of privacy.

"Where the hell have you been?" Stacey asked.

Her sister crossed her arms and glared. "Does it matter? You kicked me out."

"From the apartment, not from our lives. What about Tina? She left for the care facility earlier today and where were you? Dicking around with Jacob?"

"She's already in a home?"

"I texted you!"

"Oh. Jacob got me a new phone."

She pulled it out of her purse. It was a smartphone like everyone else seemed to have. Stacey shook her head.

"You couldn't have given me the new number?"

"I forgot," Allison said lamely.

Stacey tried not to roll her eyes. She didn't want to fight with her sister at the party, but it was proving difficult.

"Well, Tina went to the home today. You need to go see her."

"I will. I didn't know you had found a place that you could afford. Who are you even here with? I didn't see Charlie."

"I—"

Allison cut her off, smirking, "It's that Asian guy, isn't it? Your boss. You're dating him." She clicked her tongue against the roof of her mouth and shook her head.

Stacey could feel herself blush. "We aren't talking about my love life. We're talking about Tina."

"Fine. I'll drop it for now."

"Thank you."

Allison's smirk left her. "I do want to see her though. I'll give you the new number. Tell me where she is and I'll see her when Jacob can take me."

"Take you?"

"He'll send a car for me."

"Are you living with him?"

"No, no. He put me up in a hotel when I told him of my evil sister kicking me out of our home. Listen, don't start complaining. It's a blessing in disguise. Jacob was over me until I went to him about being kicked out. Now he feels as if he's my savior. It's working out really well."

What could Stacey say? She didn't understand her sister or how she could try to marry Jacob under less-than honest circumstances. Instead she just nodded. It was safer that way.

"Can we go back to the party and hash things out later?" Allison asked, already turning around.

"I guess so," Stacey mumbled.

She wanted to tell Allison more about Tina and maybe even lecture her for a bit longer. But Allison was clearly not interested. They went back to the kitchen to re-join the party and found Jacob had set up shop there, boasting about his recent trip to Europe. Tony was listening to him with a drink in his hand. Allison draped herself over Jacob and looked at him lovingly. She was a good actress.

Stacey went to stand by Tony, who looked at her. "Everything okay?"

"Yeah, it's fine. She's here with Jacob."

He raised his eyebrows. "Such a strange couple."

"Tell me about it," Stacey mumbled over Jacob's voice.

Tony leaned over to her. He was so close, she could feel his breath on her neck. For a second she thought he was going to kiss her.

But instead, he whispered, "Not in regard to your sister. I just mean with Jacob. How much do you know about him?"

"Not much," Stacey admitted.

"He got all his money from his dad. His dad is still in control of the company. They specialize in tea. They sell this crazy gourmet shit to bored rich people. So, Jacob goes around and oversees some of the offices and comes back to bore us all at these events."

"Tea?" she repeated.

"Tea."

"Geez, I figured he was involved in something a bit more interesting."

Tony laughed. His laugh sent shivers up and down her spine.

"No, just tea. But that isn't the weird part. He normally dates supermodels. Females who are way out of his dating pool but ones he can date because of his money. For him to be dating your sister is a bit unusual."

Something about his words made Stacey go on high alert. She looked at Allison and Jacob. He was still going on about something as Allison pretended to cling to his every word.

"Do you think he actually likes her?" she wondered aloud.

"I wouldn't get my hopes up."

"So, if he only dates supermodels, and he's dating my sister… well, we have to be missing something."

"I would assume so. I just don't know what."

"Just another thing to worry about," Stacey sighed.

"Don't. Your sister is a grown woman. If she wants to date Jacob, then let her."

"She only wants money. It isn't as if she really likes him."

Tony looked at her for a beat too long. Stacey wondered if he was suddenly thinking that was why she was dating him. Stacey was just about to tell him that she wasn't like that when she saw a familiar face enter the kitchen.

It was Charlie. Her heart skipped a beat and she could feel her stomach lurch. The sudden sight of him threw her off guard. Tony hadn't noticed. He had turned his attention back to Jacob.

Charlie hadn't seen her. He was stopping to say hello to some guests. She still hadn't met the owner of this house who was celebrating his birthday. The crowd was growing bigger as the night went on. Stacey suddenly felt very warm in the kitchen stuffed with people.

"I'll be right back," Stacey said to Tony.

She moved her way through the crowd and managed to reach the patio. There was a massive pool with a clear dance floor placed on top of it. People were dancing as the pool water changed colors. The music was loud and thumping. It didn't do anything to help Stacey steady her rapidly beating heart.

She cut across the yard toward the garden area. It didn't seem to be as crowded. This barely felt like a birthday party. It felt more like a giant bash. She had been expecting something quaint and light, not the sort of party she used to see on TV shows.

The garden was quieter. There were only a few people milling around. Stacey sat down on the bench and took a deep breath. The kitchen had suddenly felt so small. To see Charlie had proven to be too much.

The events of the day threatened to engulf her. She was thinking about Tina sitting in her new room, alone and without anyone she knew. Stacey should have stayed home and not come here.

"I can't believe it."

Stacey looked up and stifled a groan. In front of her, out of all the people to run into, was Adele. She was dressed in a pink dress that seemed to have been poured on. She looked radiant.

"What are you doing here?" Adele demanded. "Did you sneak in? I'll call security on you, you know."

"I didn't sneak in," Stacey snapped. "I'm here with someone."

"Of course, you are. Things go wrong with Charlie, and you just happen to find someone else you can latch onto. Some other poor unsuspecting man to mooch off."

Stacey closed her eyes. Maybe Adele was just an annoying mirage who would vanish once she opened her eyes again. She counted to three. Adele was still standing there with her hands on her hips.

"No luck," Stacey mumbled.

"What? Listen, whatever idea you have about coming here to try to win Charlie back, you can forget it."

Adele spun on her high heels and stormed off toward the house. Stacey watched her go. Was Adele here with Charlie? There was no way, she decided. Charlie had made it clear as day that he wasn't interested in Adele. That was some comfort at least.

The tightness in her chest lessened. She was feeling a little better. It didn't seem as if the walls were closing around her out here. Stacey didn't want Tony to wonder where she had gone so she headed back to the party.

The kitchen had changed little when Stacey returned. For once, Jacob was letting someone else speak for a change. A tall woman was talking about something not at all interesting. Allison shot Stacey a bored look. Stacey scanned the room for Tony.

Tony was there, talking to Charlie. She balked at the idea of joining Tony right then. But he must have sensed her because he glanced up and beckoned her over. Charlie saw her at the same moment. His back went stiff as he stared at her.

"There you are. Was wondering where you went," Tony remarked as he pulled her in for a hug.

The sudden hug felt awkward in front of Charlie. She pulled away after a few seconds. Tony swung his arm around her shoulders. He had never been this touchy-feely before and it felt strange. Charlie was looking at her without any expression on his face. She remembered seeing him the last time, storming over to his apartment and wanting him to kiss her.

"So, anyway, like I was saying. I think full coverage of the remodel of the city would be fantastic. My media companies can give you any package you want at a special price."

Charlie flicked his gaze away from Stacey and looked at Tony, "I'm guessing you would want something in return."

Tony laughed and removed his hand from Stacey's shoulders. He hit Charlie playfully on the back and turned him away from Stacey, "Well, naturally."

Tony steered Charlie away from her. Stacey watched as the crowd swallowed them up. She was alone yet again at this stupid party. She should have just bowed out. The only way this party could get worse would be if her ex-boyfriend, Jake, suddenly appeared.

She was saved from loneliness when Allison popped up at her side.

"Hey, I ditched Jacob for the moment. Wanna look around?"

"Are you allowed out of his sight for more than one second?" Stacey joked.

"He's boring some woman in the kitchen. Besides, I saw you standing here completely out of your comfort zone as your ex and your current fuck strolled away together."

"Geez, Allison, still so crass."

"Not going to change. Come on. Let's go upstairs." She grabbed Stacey's hand.

"We aren't allowed upstairs, are we?" she protested.

Allison rolled her eyes, "Which is the exact reason why we are going upstairs."

Stacey didn't have any fight left in her to protest. As Allison dragged her through the crowd, she saw Tony enter the room again. He was looking for her. Charlie was gone. Whatever conversation they had was apparently extremely short. She didn't see Charlie anywhere in the vicinity.

Normally, she would have pulled away from Allison and gone to Tony. But she was exhausted having to deal with people. She was secretly relieved her sister was here. Allison yanked her out of the room and into a hallway.

"The staircase is over—"

"Geez, we aren't going to use the main one. I heard this guy has a bowling alley and I want to see it."

Allison stopped at a thin wooden door. She looked around and opened it. There was a narrow staircase that led upstairs. She looked at Stacey.

"Cool, right?"

"It is sorta cool. How did you know about it?"

"Jacob talks a lot. Come on."

Allison went up the stairs. Stacey glanced around and followed her. The staircase looked like it was used for service or maintenance staff. They opened another small door at the top and stepped out into a hallway upstairs.

"Nothing remarkable here," Stacey remarked.

"Well, what were you expecting? A portal to another universe?" Allison huffed and took off down the hallway.

She stopped to peek into each room. Most of them were bedrooms that were unused. There was seemingly no one else up there. There was a room filled with paintings and statues that were shoved in randomly.

"Probably wants to sell this shit," Allison said before moving on.

At the next door, Stacey noticed it was slightly ajar. But Allison didn't notice. She pushed it open before Stacey could say anything. She heard her sister let out a gasp of surprise. Stacey pushed past her. Her heart fell.

Adele and Charlie were on the bed. Adele's arms were wrapped around Charlie, while her lips were on his mouth. He was on top of her. It was fortunate that they were still fully clothed.

Even so, Stacey felt the shock roll through her. She blindly turned away as the lovers noticed they had been caught.

It was a mistake to come to this party after all.

-To be continued in Book 3-

If you enjoyed this title, I would appreciate your leaving a review of the book. Good reviews encourage an author to write as well as help books to sell. Good reviews can be just a few short sentences describing what you liked about the book without having a spoiler. If you could spend 30 seconds writing a review, I would appreciate it: you can review this title right now at your favorite retailer.

Here is a preview of the **next book** you may also enjoy:

THE NEXT few seconds seemed to be a complete blur. As soon as Stacey saw Adele's lips on Charlie, she had turned around blindly and left the room. She had to get out of there right that instant. The last thing she wanted to do was cry. There was no point in crying; she had broken up with Charlie. If he wanted to finally fool around with Adele, then let him.

Allison said something, but Stacey didn't hear it. She was practically jogging down the hallway to the staircase. Allison was hot on her heels. Stacey didn't want to turn around and see if Charlie had followed her or not.

Down the stairs she went. She spilled out into the party and started weaving through the crowd. She was halfway to the entrance when someone grabbed her arm. Startled, she let out a cry and turned around.

It was Tony. It took Stacey a couple of seconds to remember that she had come to the party with him.

"There you are!"

"Uh, yeah, here I am," she mumbled and scanned the crowd for Charlie.

"Listen, come with me to the patio. There is –"

"I can't. I'm sorry." She shook her head. "I have to go. I have a massive headache and I'm in a lot of pain."

Concern flickered across his face, along with something else that Stacey couldn't put her finger on. Tony let go of her. Someone bumped into her as they walked by. The party seemed to have doubled in size in the short time Stacey had been upstairs.

"Thanks for inviting me," she said quickly.

"Wait, how are you getting home?" Tony called after her as she left.

"I'll call a cab!"

She pushed her way through the crowd and out of the front door. Even here the crowd was thick. Her frantic state was starting to mix with feelings of claustrophobia from the mass of bodies surrounding her on all sides. She was on the verge of either passing out or bursting into tears if she didn't get out of this place quickly.

Stacey took off down the driveway toward the gate. Tears were pressing against her eyes. She cursed herself for acting so stupidly. How could she be so upset? She had opted out of dealing with Charlie and his family drama. She had no right to be so upset.

"There you are!"

Stacey froze for a second. But it was enough for Charlie to grab her arm exactly where Tony had. He turned her around. Her heart began to beat rapidly at the sight of him. Music was pouring out of the house. She could hear the heavy beats of the bass even out here on the driveway. The lights from the house seemed to illuminate Charlie from behind. He glowed softly.

"Stacey, let me explain."

"You don't have to explain. It isn't any of my business."

"I'm trying to move on."

Stacey was brought up short. The words swirled in her head. She hadn't been expecting for Charlie to say that.

Taking advantage of her silence, he said, "We're over. I mean, you made it clear. Then Tony tells me you two are dating. I can't really sit around and pine for you any longer, can I?"

"No. I guess not."

"So, Adele was interested and I had never given her a chance before because of my father. So I thought I would."

"Isn't that falling directly into what your father wants?" Stacey asked.

Charlie shrugged. "Maybe. I guess so. I don't care, Stacey. I'm tired. Fighting against my dad like this is downright exhausting. I don't want to do it any longer."

Stacey couldn't keep the bitter tone out of her voice. "So, you'll just date her because she's around and your father already approves."

"No, no, you don't get to do this." He shook his head. "*You* left. You left *me*, remember? Now that I'm moving on, you don't get to be angry about it."

"I'm not angry."

"Yes, you are. Did you expect me to just be miserable for the rest of my life?"

"I expected you to reach out to me after I broke up with you!" Stacey snapped. "You seemed completely fine with the fact I had dumped you. And out of all the people to move on with, you pick Adele. The same woman you made clear that you had no interest in!"

"It doesn't concern you, Stacey! What I do now isn't any of your business! As for why I didn't contact you, I thought that was what you wanted! You broke up with me! I wasn't going to crawl around after you because you didn't want me any longer."

The two of them stared at each other. Charlie's eyes were wide. He had shifted in the middle of his rant. Half of his face was covered in shadows now. Behind him, Stacey could see Adele breaking through the edge of the crowd.

"Maybe you were right," Charlie whispered.

"About what?"

"Maybe we are just from two different worlds."

Stacey felt the air get sucked from her lungs at Charlie's words. She didn't have a chance to reply.

Adele had slinked up to Charlie. She wrapped her arms around his waist and rested her chin on his shoulder.

"Everything okay?"

"Yes. I'm just going, actually. Have a good night," Stacey replied stiffly.

She turned around and headed toward the gate, leaving Charlie behind.

If you enjoyed this sample then look for **Love Reinstated: Persuasive Billionaire BWWM Romance Series, Book 3**.

Here is a preview of **another story** you may enjoy:

"**THEY WANT** them Black Forest cheesecakes done in thirty," Melanie said, chewing on a stick of gum.

Adalia sighed and blinked a couple times. "I'm not a miracle worker. Besides, I hardly think anyone in the store is going to riot if I don't get it out on time."

Annie's Market specialized in nothing but providing loads of baked goods to as many customers as possible – in short, the quality was terrible. The recipes in the bakery section were set and Adalia's creativity was stifled, but a job was a job and God knew she needed the money after that debauchery with Trent.

Melanie shuffled out of the kitchen and the doors swung in her wake. The girl had about as much finesse as a bull on steroids. She'd worked there for a week as Adalia's manager, and it was difficult to respect her.

Failure, failure, failure. The word repeated itself in her head.

Measure out the flour, *failure*, weigh the sugar, *failure*, beat the eggs, *failure*. It didn't matter what she did or which way she looked at things. She'd messed up. Big time.

Melanie shoved back into the kitchen. "Store manager says to get 'em done or you're in trouble."

"You went to the store manager?" Adalia stared at her and shook her head.

"Yeah, and there's some guy here to see you."

Adalia's heart leapt into her throat, and she stopped moving completely. Screw the Black Forest cakes, what if Trent had arrived? Mortification paralyzed her; she was glued to the spot.

The last thing she'd want was the billionaire to see her slumming it in a tiny store bakery.

"Who?" Adalia whispered.

Melanie raised an eyebrow. "Derick or something, I didn't hear proper. Get them cakes ready." She turned and charged out again, still chewing gum like it was her air to breathe.

"Derick," Adalia said to herself, shaking her head in confusion. Who the hell was Derick? She dusted off her hands on her grubby apron and strolled out of the kitchen and into the kiosk area.

It wasn't Derick; it was DeShawn.

"Hey baby," he murmured, resting his elbows on top of the glass case, and gazing into her eyes. "I've been thinking about you all day."

"I'm honored," she replied, and the sarcasm was lost on him. She didn't want to see Trent, but she surely didn't want to see her ex-boyfriend either. He'd pretty much messed with her mind for long enough, and she didn't need that added pressure or drama.

"You working here now?"

"No," she grumbled. "I just come here to work out."

"Huh?"

"Nothing," she said with a sweet smile. "What do you want, DeShawn? I've got things to do right now." She glanced out over the empty store and made eye contact with the manager.

He glared at her and tilted his head to the side like the oversized buzzard he was. "Hurry up," he mouthed then tapped his cheap Kmart watch.

She forced herself not to roll her eyes at the authority figure. Once upon a time, she'd loved baking, but that was when she'd been able to create something from fresh, not stick to the plan, no matter how disgusting it was.

"Baby?" DeShawn's voice interrupted her train of thought.

"What is it?" She snapped her focus back to his face. "Like I said, I'm busy."

"And I said I want you back."

Agony erupted in her chest, pushing aside every other emotion. She'd been through so much, tasted a hint of success and then fallen hard. All she wanted was to get back on her feet and move on with her life, but DeShawn was back.

"Why? Give me one good reason why."

"Because I love you, baby," he said, leaning over the case of day-old cakes to grab at her arm. She didn't jerk it away and he managed to bring it up and take hold of her hand instead. He brought the tips of her fingers to his lips and kissed them gently.

There wasn't heat like there was with Trent, but it still brought out something in her. Something good. A long forgotten memory of what it was like to be touched by a person who cared.

Did DeShawn truly care?

"I don't trust you, and I don't need that," she said, pulling her hand from his grasp and wiping the back on her apron with a sour expression.

"You never gave me a chance to prove myself to you. I love you so much, baby, and you ain't never given me the chance to show it."

"What are you talking about?" she spat, trembling from head to toe. "I gave you every chance in the world to show your love for me and you didn't make any effort whatsoever."

"I came to your daddy's place to talk to you."

"What?!" Adalia laughed out loud and the manager shot her a look of pure loathing. "I'm not talking about after I dumped your sorry ass. By then, it was too late. I'm talking about before. Because when it really mattered, you didn't give a crap."

"I was high a lot of the time."

"Precisely." Adalia gripped the low-slung counter with both hands.

Melanie appeared beside her. "You gotta get back to work. The Black Forest cakes aren't gonna bake themselves."

"What the hell does a store need two managers for?" Adalia blurted, then snapped her mouth shut.

Melanie glared at her for a minute then charged off again, muttering to herself.

That meant more trouble for her. The bakery manager chewed and steamed her way over to the store manager and flung her arms around, describing what Adalia had said in minute detail, apparently.

"You realize how busy I am, right?" Adalia breathed slowly, through the anger and disappointment in herself.

"Yeah, true that. Look, girl, I can't live without you. I'm not gonna treat you bad again. Only give you what you deserve. You gotta believe me."

If you enjoyed this sample then look for **Love Forgiven: Tenacious Billionaire BWWM Romance Series, Book 2**.

Here is a preview of **another story** you may enjoy:

Love Evaded: Ardent Billionaire Romance Series, Book 2

"DEIRDRE, I love that new top." Cassie grinned as Deirdre walked out of the bathroom. It was a Friday night and Deirdre had a date with her new boyfriend, Felix.

"Thanks Cass," Deirdre answered, smoothing the silk fabric of her new peach tunic. The color looked amazing against Deirdre's skin; her plain, black slacks and ballet flats completed the outfit nicely.

"Where is Felix taking you?"

"We're going to try that new Thai place, near the college," Deirdre explained. "Felix has a late class tonight, so I'm meeting him there.

Deirdre had met Felix at the art college where she posed for classes. She'd started by modeling for hobby photographers, but over the last several weeks she'd sat for painters, sketch artists, and sculptors. She'd been offered the job after she'd gone to Simon, the photography instructor, and told him about the teenager at the hibachi restaurant who'd somehow ended up with one of her nude photos.

Simon had been outraged, and had assigned his graduate student Felix to get to the bottom of the situation. Felix had researched everyone in the hobby class, and found that only one had a teenaged son. Simon himself had visited the middle-aged student, and alerted him to the fact that his son was going through his things. The instructor left with all of Deirdre's photos; Felix had gathered photos from the rest of the students, to ensure that Deirdre would never be put in that position again. Simon changed his class policies; only works that didn't depict the model's face could be kept by their creators. Most of the students were sympathetic to the reasons behind the new policy, and many began sketching and painting the faces of their classmates onto Deirdre's body.

After the new policy went into effect, Deirdre happily agreed to pose whenever Simon needed her. On her second trip to the school, Felix asked her out on a date. The graduate student was kind, genuine and thoughtful, and Deirdre hated herself for thinking of Parker Hamlin when she was with him.

A month had passed since the last time she'd seen the gorgeous billionaire, but his face still haunted her thoughts. That morning at his studio, she'd been convinced that he was falling in love with her. She'd already allowed herself to fall in love with him. But then, just as she'd feared, he'd decided that she wasn't the type of person he wanted to be with. Ironically, the job that had brought her to Felix was the same job that had made Parker walk away. Deirdre still wondered what her life would be like now if they hadn't run into that teenager. She sighed out loud.

"What's the matter, Dee?" Cassie asked knowingly.

"Nothing," she replied quickly. Deirdre knew exactly what her best friend would say if she knew that Parker was still in her thoughts.

"Are you sure? You seem distracted… pensive even."

"I'm just stressed about school, Cass," Deirdre assured her. "I feel like I'm never going to finish."

"It'll take as long as it takes, Dee. It doesn't matter when you graduate. It just matters that you keep working at it."

"That's nice of you to say, but it does matter. The sooner I finish school, the sooner I can get a better job and move D'Angelo to a better neighborhood." Thoughts of her brother's safety were always at the forefront of Deirdre's mind.

"You'll feel better next semester," Cassie assured her, "when you're on campus."

Deirdre smiled at the thought of going to real, live lectures as opposed to online classes. She'd managed to land another weekly singing gig that paid better than her Thursdays at Fuseli's. That, combined with her regular modeling sessions at the art college, had made it possible for her to quit her job at the hotel. She'd be able to spend most of the summer home with D'Angelo, and start classes on campus in August.

"Would you have ever thought that my saving grace would come from Carl?" Deirdre laughed. Her ex-boyfriend Carl had been the one who had found her the modeling job.

"Yeah, I bet if he'd known you'd hook-up with Felix, he'd have never set you up in the job." Cassie laughed. "But that's Carl for you. He never thinks things through. I still can't believe what happened to him."

Deirdre nodded. Towards the end of her relationship with Carl, she'd suspected that he was involved with one of the local gangs. After she left him, he'd stopped trying to hide what he was up to. He'd even tried to use her apartment as a stash pad for his illegal activities. Deirdre had refused, and two weeks ago Carl had been arrested for possession of stolen goods and a laundry list of illegal substances. The other gang members were perfectly happy to let Carl take the fall, and word on the street was that he was looking at forty years in a federal penitentiary.

"Maybe he and my mother can reconnect," Deirdre said flatly.

"Have you talked to her recently?" Cassie pressed. Deirdre hardly ever talked about her mother, and talked to her even less.

"I send her pictures of D'Angelo. He used to write letters to send along with them, but he doesn't anymore. She writes once a week… apologizes, says she's changed. She's even found God, apparently. But I don't have anything to say to her."

"Well, we have more important things to think about, don't we?" Cassie smiled. She'd been friends with Deirdre since grade school, and was almost as hurt by Pauline's drug use as her children were. "You need to get going, you don't want to make Felix wait."

Deirdre took one last look in the mirror, kissed D'Angelo goodbye, and rushed out the door.

Deirdre arrived at the small, storefront restaurant and saw Felix's Audi already in the parking lot. She walked through the door and found him sitting at a small, private booth near the back wall. She smiled broadly as she walked over to join him, and he rose to greet her.

"You look beautiful." He smiled as he leaned down and kissed her cheek.

"Thanks," she offered graciously, "how was your class?"

Felix sighed. "It's a freshman level humanities class… no one is there because they want to be, they're there because they have to be. And that includes yours truly." He shrugged.

Deirdre sat across the table, studying her date. Felix was tall and lanky, with blue eyes and curly auburn hair that hung down over his ears. He was attractive in that free-spirited, down-to-earth way. Felix was in his final year of the art college's Masters of Arts program. An artistic genius, he'd attended a progressive liberal arts high school that allowed him to take college art courses. He'd received his bachelor's degree just one year after officially graduating high school; he was on track to finish his master's degree at only twenty-two.

"I'll be teaching what I want to teach soon enough." Felix smiled. "How has your day been? How was D'Angelo's awards assembly?"

Deirdre smiled, surprised that he'd remembered. The last day of school awards assembly at D'Angelo's school had been that morning. Deirdre had mentioned it to Felix only once, and that had been at least two weeks ago.

"It was fantastic." She beamed. "D'Angelo got the Presidential Award for Academic Excellence, and also the Presidential Fitness award. He was the only one in his class who got both. He's ready to make you pay up on his report card too, he has straight A's."

Felix whistled. "And I said ten bucks an A, right? I may have to renegotiate my price for next year or that kid is going to break me," he teased.

Deirdre felt incredibly lucky to have found Felix, if for no other reason than the fact that he was so good with D'Angelo. Felix had lost his own parents in a car accident when he was ten, and afterward his older brother and sister-in-law had raised him. He understood the boy's situation better than Deirdre could ever hope to.

If you enjoyed this sample then look for **Love Evaded - Ardent Billionaire Romance Series, Book 2.**

Other Books by Shyla Starr

- Tenacious Billionaire BWWM Romance Series

- Elusive Billionaire Romance Series

- Lonely Billionaire Romance Series

- Ardent Billionaire Romance Series

- Fervent Billionaire BWWM Romance Series

- Audacious Billionaire BWWM Romance Series

Get the latest update on new releases from the author at:

https://shylastarr.com/newsletter/

About the Author - Shyla Starr

Shyla currently specializes in writing interracial romance stories and is a huge fan of the alpha male. Simply put, there just aren't enough stories about mixed couple romances, which is something she is aiming to fix.

Being a bookworm all her life, when Shyla discovered men she also realized how easy it was to fulfill her fantasies through her writing.

When not writing and fantasizing about men, Shyla enjoys dancing, reading and chilling with her friends.

Connect with Shyla Starr

I really appreciate you reading my book! Here are my social media coordinates:

Friend me on Facebook:
https://www.facebook.com/shylastarrauthor

Follow me on Twitter: https://twitter.com/shylstarr

Check me out on Goodreads:
https://www.goodreads.com/author/show/8436084.Shyla_Starr

Subscribe to my newsletter:
https://shylastarr.com/newsletter/

Visit my website: https://shylastarr.com/